his in the fire

WWINTERS

His in the Fire
Copyright © 2026 Willow Winters Publishing
All rights reserved.

No part of this publication may be reproduced, stored in a retrieval system, or transmitted in any form or by any means, electronic, mechanical, photocopying, recording, scanning, or otherwise, without the prior written permission of the publisher, except in the case of brief quotations within critical reviews and otherwise as permitted by copyright law.

NOTE: This is a work of fiction.

Names, characters, places, and incidents are a product of the author's imagination.

Any resemblance to real life is purely coincidental. All characters in this story are 18 or older.

Persephone

Ripped away from Olympus to the Underworld was a hell of its own making, but so is returning. Leaving behind Hades and my rightful place as queen of the Underworld caused an agony I've never known before.

What's worse is that the war has not come to an end, and my place in Olympus is questioned by all because of Hades's demands. My mother will stop at nothing to have me safe with her and neither will Hades.

I'm left torn between Olympus, my mother, and the throne I was always meant to have beside my lover, the king of the dead. I miss him dearly, I crave his touch, and I need the love I felt so strongly in his presence.

What brings me the most fear though, are my own thoughts and my own power. The threat of losing what I had is enough to make me question my sanity. My mother would starve the world for me, Hades would burn it. But me… What I'm willing to do as the suffering intensifies is blasphemy and terrifies me to my core.
There's no going back and in this place, I must find peace and balance before it's too late.

I know one thing for certain: after dark there will always be light. If that wasn't true, the dark would not have a name…
And I crave both.

playlist

Little Girl Gone - Chinchilla

Lily - Alan Walker, K-391

Light Em' Up - Fall Out Boy

Bones - Imagine Dragons

Take me to church - Hozier

You Give Love A Bad Name - Bon Jovi

Sweet Dreams - Eurythmics

his
in
the
fire

chapter 1

Persephone

OLYMPUS IS BLINDING.

The shoes click on the white marble floor with every step I take, and I can barely breathe. Hecate's hand protectively around my arm holds me close, and I...I can't see. It is the brightest light I have ever encountered. One moment, I was in the Underworld and the next, the mother of crossroads and keeper of the keys has taken me home.

I cover my eyes with a stifled gasp as my legs find grounding. Hecate's grip tightens, but only so much that I may rely on her for support. She's strong. I've always known such things, but now I can feel her power in her touch.

She pauses as my body stiffens and I heave in a breath, my head light.

Her eyes are vacant as I look up to her and yet they hold so many memories.

"Are you well?" Hecate whispers. Her voice echoes as if I've heard it three times. The mother, the maiden, the crone. All of her is concerned.

"Yes," I answer in a hushed tone. I am *not* well though. My heart screams the truth. My soul is torn and where I belong is unknown to me. Fate has meant to torture me.

Her eyes flash as if she knows. As if she can hear every thought that races through me.

Unable to meet her gaze, my eyes adjust to my surroundings. Olympus.

Everything has changed during my time in the Underworld. I found myself there, my power and my strength. I learned to live without the fear of what was to come, and now I have been ripped away. Or rather I ripped myself away.

The words Hades and Hecate spoke ring in my ears. The words she said to me:

No magic will save you now. You must come back to the world that is now forever changed.

We have both changed, I answered, and now I know it is true. The girl I was before I went to the Underworld would never have found the light of Olympus to be so harsh.

And what Hades said to Hecate...

Do not leave her side. Do not betray me.

His own words were a betrayal to me, though. I'd

fallen for him, truly and deeply. And yet he spoke in front of me as though there were conversations I may not partake in. Could he have made a deal with Hecate about me? Did they have some understanding before Hecate appeared in the Underworld?

You have betrayed me. That was what Hecate replied. I am no fool. There were conversations Hades participated in that I was not privy to. It all happened too fast. I was kept in the dark, and resentment bleeds in slowly with that knowledge.

Why didn't Hades tell me? The memory of his voice sends chills through me.

Hecate is coming. There is too much death, my queen. The gods have created an imbalance.

My mind spins with these revelations. I inhale deeply. I will not allow myself to slip into feeling small. That is how I felt when I discovered I had been taken to the Underworld, and it cost me days I could have done more with. Instead, those days were filled with tears and despair.

"Are you sure?" Hecate questions. My gaze searches hers. Comfort lies beyond her concern. As if this is meant to be.

"It is...very bright," I manage to say, my eyes stinging as they adjust. "And the Underworld..." I whisper, unable to complete the thought. It was chaos in the Underworld. Parts of Hades's realms collapsed, crumbling as I watched. Souls poured through the sky above us, and Hades moved through the vast space so quickly

I could not fathom the power it must have taken. "I cannot see. I need a moment to adjust."

Her grip loosens only so she may hold my hand as I come to terms with all that has happened.

I crave to go back to Hades. For him to stand at my side. I need to go back to my power, to the rooms I had grown used to, and to the magic I had been working on.

My magic. My heart stutters, and the doubt I once felt returns only to fall silent to the ringing in my ears.

The marble remains steady under my feet.

I blink slowly, forcing myself to stare at the floor. Even the floor is bright with light reflecting off it. It is a strange light, though.

The room Hecate and I are standing in is spacious and cool, but it looks out on a courtyard with white smoke drifting through it. A large pot has been tipped over and cracked, its pieces lying scattered where it fell. There is more smoke wafting above the roof.

Hecate must see my shock, because her grip gets gentler. "You have nothing to fear, Persephone."

I turn my attention to her. *Don't I?* I want to ask. War came to the Underworld because of me. I was taken, then stolen back. My father could have spoken with Hades, could have dealt with him without so much destruction, but he did not.

I do not speak the question aloud. It is not something I want to voice when I have no idea who may be listening, or who is responsible for what.

"I would not lie to you," she says and again her voice

seems to echo twice. All three of her reassure me. "Fear does not belong to you, so release it."

I nod, although I don't do so consciously. At the thought, as if under a spell, the fear trickles away. Emotions dim as logic replaces it. What has happened is gone. What will come is not here yet. My feet are planted in the present and I stand with Hecate at the crossroads of the living and the dead.

Hecate studies my eyes, then gives a shallow nod.

"Are you in need of anything?" she asks. "Food? Drink?"

"I am not. Thank you." I could eat, but it would replace the taste of the pomegranate seeds that still lingers on my tongue. The decadent fruit and memory of Hades. In the harsh light of Olympus, it feels like the Underworld might have been some kind of dream.

It was *not* a dream, I reassure myself. It was real. I'm disoriented because I have spent so much time in the Underworld, but I'm not powerless. Not anymore.

Hecate takes me at my word and releases me entirely as if she was only holding on to steady me for the journey. Was that what it was like to travel to the Underworld? I suppose I would not have noticed. To me, it felt like falling into a cold, dark sleep.

Somehow, I did not think the light would feel colder, but it does. So much colder than I remember.

I follow Hecate out of the room, our steps slow but steady and across the vacant courtyard. The once lively state is far too empty for my liking. Distant voices echo in the halls, and shadows move from room to room. What *happened* here? I witnessed the souls streaming into the Underworld, but they had to have come from the mortal realm, not Olympus.

Did the battle rage here, too?

Impossible.

"Where is my father?" I question as alarm wraps itself around my shoulders. My pace quickens as I realize the time passed has been unkind to Olympus.

"We are headed to him now," she says, and unfortunately my anxiousness only intensifies.

Hecate does not seem surprised by the quiet murmurs and the soft, rushing footsteps as we walk. She nods to a few servants who bow as we make our way through the halls. We stop once or twice only to let them pass.

My body quivers as we get closer.

I cannot get my bearings. I know these halls. I grew up on the grounds of Olympus. All my childhood memories were bathed in this light. Now it all feels unfamiliar, as if it rearranged itself while I was gone. As if it wanted to be something new when I returned.

Perhaps it is only a consequence of moving between realms.

Perhaps, I think, *I* am the one who is new and different, and suddenly these bright halls do not seem endless. They do not seem like a dream. They are not the place my heart aches for.

Hecate stops outside a beautifully carved quartz

archway. It takes me a few beats to realize that this is the archway leading to my rooms.

My rooms. The ones I spent so much time in. The ones I whispered my worries to Beatrice in. The ones I set up altars in, begging for help with my magic.

The ones I was stolen from.

"Would you like to change?" Hecate questions delicately. It takes a moment for her question to register.

I glance at my simple linen gown.

My heart thumps a little harder. There are conversations that will need to be had. What does it matter what I wear? There are much more important matters at hand.

Goosebumps run down my arms.

Do not drink the wine. Tell me you understand, Hades said, just before Hecate appeared.

I will not drink the wine, I promised Hades.

I draw myself up and answer, "I will change later, if need be. Is my mother waiting for me?" My mother. I need her so. I need her now.

"She will return soon," Hecate answers. "It is your father who wishes to see you and who you must see first." Disappointment runs through me for only a moment.

I wonder about that as we walk through the halls. Olympus is teeming with servants. There are more than usual, or else they have all been called to help with whatever disaster happened here. Some kind of storm? An argument between gods?

I am certain I will find out.

It strikes me again that I am walking next to Hecate.

Hecate, who I have prayed to so many times. Who I have begged for help in my darkest moments. Who Beatrice often relies on.

I steal a glance at her out of the corner of my eye. Her dark robes flow, sinuous against the white walls. She holds her head high. A subtle breeze, like magic, stirs her long dark hair.

She is regal and unmovable.

For a moment, I feel like a girl walking next to her—young and fearful that I would lose my powers and helpless to do anything about it.

But I straighten my back. I stand tall beside her.

I am a queen in my own right.

Is it your own right? My inner voice questions. *Will you ever be allowed to return?*

My throat tightens at the thought. I must return. Hades looked into my eyes and swore that his love would last forever. *Forever,* to the gods, is not a small thing. He intends for me to be his queen for all eternity.

Then what am I doing *here,* on Olympus? *My mother.* I need my mother.

It does not take long for us to reach the grand main hall. The doors open before us, and I step through with Hecate.

My father sits on his throne on the massive dais, and as I enter, he picks up his head. His eyes wide with surprise. They flash as he registers me and the delight and welcoming arms are unexpected.

A softness runs through me.

He rises from the throne and comes to me, his pace fast, his strides long, his arms outstretched. When he reaches me, he folds me in a tight hug. And I rest in his hold, feeling as if I belong. As if I've found love that I'd lost.

Hushed murmurs rise in the background.

With a prick on the back of my neck I can feel the eyes of Olympus watching. The main hall is not empty. There is an audience.

Finally, my father pulls back, his hands cupping my shoulders. "Persephone. Are you well?"

"I am," I answer easily.

"And your journey was a safe one?" he questions, but I'm unable to answer.

"It was safe indeed, Zeus," Hecate states. Her tone colder than it was with me.

"My daughter has returned to us," my father announces, and scattered cheers go up from the others in the main hall. He looks down and studies my face again. Applause fills the hall and white gowns appear from the corner of my eyes.

Thoughts of my sisters bombard me. I'd forgotten how much I'd lost while in the Underworld. Slowly, I come back to who I was before and I find love there.

"You're sure you are well?" My father's eyes pry into my own. An urge to pull away takes over and I do just that, then I grab his hands with my own and hold them between us. The rough calluses caused by his bolts make me aware of just how soft my own hands are.

"Of course, Father," I tell him. "I am well."

His brow furrows. "You were not injured? Forced?"

I shake my head. I do not know how to answer him. My first weeks in the Underworld were harrowing, but that was because I was not ready to see it for what it was.

A new world. A whole realm.

With a king at the center of it. And a place for my power.

I can barely look him in the eyes. I know not what to tell. Especially with prying eyes and so many who will hear. I must be careful.

My voice is calm but low as I recount to the court. "I left my rooms. It felt like falling into a dream, and when I woke, I was somewhere else."

My father looks solemnly into my eyes, the corner of his mouth turning down. "Stolen in the night. But you are unharmed?"

"I have not been harmed, Father."

My father exhales, as if he is relieved.

"I am glad you were not harmed," he says, pulling me close again. "You have the favor of the Fates."

The Fates…just the thought of them brings back flashes of a memory.

I do not know if I have their favor, but I *was* given advice.

You may thrive in death as much as you would have in life, they said, in that voice that seemed to come from all of them at once. *As much in the Underworld as you can on Olympus. But neither life would be complete.*

How am I to be complete, then? I asked.

To simply be, they answered. *You do not need to choose.*

Chills flow down my shoulders now as they did then.

Once again, my father steps back. He smooths his hand over my hair. He has a soft expression on his face, but a hard glint in his eyes, as if there is something about me he cannot explain.

There is likely *much* about me that he cannot explain. Does he think I spent my time in the Underworld isolated and caged?

"I have questions," I tell him firmly.

"I will answer all in time, but—"

"Where is my mother?" I question, not allowing him to finish. A hush falls around us, and my father doesn't answer me.

"Persephone," my father says in a low, careful tone. "My daughter. I need to know. Did you eat the food in the Underworld?"

"I wasn't starved, if that is what you mean."

He glances at Hecate, who says nothing.

"I mean…" My father hesitates. This, too, seems false. When has he ever hesitated like this before? It is never because he is unsure of his thoughts. It is always done because he wishes to give a particular impression. It didn't seem quite so obvious before I went to the Underworld. "Did you eat the seeds of the pomegranate?"

His face does not change once he asks, and that is how I know.

This is the thing that matters to him. The

pomegranate seeds. They hold some importance. A *great* importance, if my father's neutral expression means what I think it does.

I look directly into his eyes, aware of everyone watching. Aware of Hecate, who already knows.

"Yes." I do not shout, but I use a clear tone, so that anyone who is listening to our conversation can hear, and there will be no mistake about what I have said. "I ate six of the pomegranate seeds."

It is then and only then that the lights dim in favor of a stormy sky. His expression morphs to one of concern and the murmurs return, not nearly as hushed as they should be for the concern that suffocates the air.

chapter 2

Hades

I AM NOTHING WITHOUT MY PERSEPHONE.

Nothing.

The pieces inside of me are hollow and empty. A shell of what I once was.

My power is meaningless without her beside me.

Anger and contempt are all that remain. My self-control has nearly gone. All the rage I have held inside me for so many years threatens to unleash itself on any poor soul who dares confront me.

I cannot tolerate this feeling. This emptiness. The places where she should be. She is missing from everywhere I look. She should be *there,* at the table. She should be *there,* in the bed. She should be *there,* in the hall.

She should be by my side. At this very moment, I need her.

Persephone should be kneeling at the grate, her gaze glinting at the magic she has worked.

Persephone should be pacing the room, a book in her hands, reading as she walks.

Persephone's enchantments should still hold, but the bell she spelled to the door has fallen silent.

It has no one to protect anymore. The chill in the air notes her absence.

I cannot stand this room and leave it without looking at the bell.

I cannot tolerate being without her. I should've fought my way out of the Underworld. I should've gone to Olympus and shattered all its pretty white columns. I should've reached to every other realm, pulled it into the Underworld, and made it mine if that's what it takes to have her.

Fate betrays me as I cannot. It is not possible to cross the realms. A sickness settles deep in my gut as my hands tremble with anger at my own doing.

I cannot do those things, and it does far more than infuriate me.

It makes me *grieve*. An emotion I have never felt.

She is lost to me. I cannot speak to her. I cannot touch her. I cannot even see her. As I stare into the abyss, I ignore the remaining screams, although they have slowed. Instead I focus on the memory of her touch and her voice and the beauty of her very existence.

I crave her. I've never desired anything. I knew not what it was to want.

It's worse than losing my power. It is worse than losing my title. Sharper than any pain I have felt.

It is worse than war.

I stalk through the halls of my home, Cerberus at my side. He butts his noses against my leg and goes ahead of me so he can get underfoot, letting out low, worried barks until I drop to one knee near one of the garden exits.

"It's all right," I tell Cerberus, stroking the ears of one head, then the next, then the next. "It will be all right."

I'm lying through my teeth, and Cerberus seems to know that, because he whines again.

Does he miss her as I do? Does he know that I cannot live without her?

I cannot say. But I do not want him to witness what will come next if she does not return as promised. Patience is a virtue that betrays me with this grief.

I get to my feet and move, ordering Cerberus to stay behind.

There is still unrest in the Underworld. Still crashes of rock and violent winds and souls lighting up the sky, crying out as they go.

I storm through my realm. I can barely control my fury. My teeth clench; my muscles coil, begging me to tear the ground apart. Destroy everything that meets my eyes. What does it matter without Persephone?

We had a deal. The betrayal only threatens the belief that she will return.

I picture her face as she turned to look at me, one

final time before Hecate took her away. Her beauty and innocence are unmatched.

I wish I had given her more morsels of the truth I know.

If she does not return, there will only be one realm. And I will rule it in its entirety.

They wish for me to live in a hell of my own making.

The gods have created an imbalance.

If they do not return her… Anger bristles. I'd rather they destroy my own soul than to live a single moment of peace knowing she is not by my side.

She is *my queen*, and I cannot even speak to her!

I let out a howl of pure anger. It's rough on my throat, burning as it leaves me. I thought my self-control was already gone, but *now* it is splitting. *Now* it is crumbling under the force of my loss. The demons of the realm return the howl. Ready for war. Ready to fight where I command them to.

Persephone should never have had to leave. A queen should never have to leave her realm.

It is a cruel trick that she has.

A trick I have, in part, played on myself.

My own mind seems to split from the pain of what was and what could have been. What should be. Again, my body trembles, the power within me barely contained.

Crazed perhaps. Will I lose my mind without her?

I love her. I spoke the words. She knows, and now she will have that truth with her in Olympus, where it is dangerous.

Deadly.

I turn around on the path simply needing to move. Every hall is suffocating. I've been moving without paying attention and have crossed great swaths of my realms, leaving me alone in a wide, foggy field. The place of a thousand years of memories.

This is not where I need to be.

I need to be at Persephone's side, with her hand in mine and our realms spread out before us, but I cannot go to her.

Instead, I go to the river.

My realms blur as I move through them again. My heart pounds and what rushes through my veins is not blood. It must be oil or acid. It feels like it should melt through me, reducing me to nothing, but it does not.

I let out a horrible, bitter laugh. Of *course* this feeling will not kill me. Of course I will keep surviving. I did that before when I had no hope of seeing the sun, and I will do it now, against my fucking will.

In the meantime, someone else will pay. *Anyone* else.

I set my sights on the vision before me. The banks of the river teem with souls. The blue hues seem to melt together. The souls in the water fade to a gray as the life leaves them, and on the shore, pushing past one another, confused and looking for comfort. Searching for peace and an end to their suffering.

I am not here to comfort them.

I lunge at the nearest souls, hate and grief overwhelming me completely. If I cannot have Persephone, these souls will not have a life in the Underworld. If I am to be denied the only touch I have been able to stomach in a thousand years, then I will deny them *everything*.

I rip souls in two with my bare hands. Ash coats the roughness of my palms as they fall to pieces beneath me. The souls are less substantial than their mortal bodies, but not by much. This is why the Fates carry shears. Most souls have strength in them—a strength that grew from their will to survive in their mortal existence.

The cord of their strength resists being cut. It fights against the shears, too, but the Fates are determined.

I am not determined. I am *obsessed*. I cannot see past this pain. It is red and black. The color of fire. The sound of a scream. Is that the souls, or does the wretched sound come from me?

I do not care. I do not need to know either.

Demeter and Zeus are not the only gods who can create an *imbalance*. It is within my power too, and they would do well to remember that. I picture them as I end the souls' existence before me. They will pay for this pain. If they do not return her, I will allow the imbalance to destroy us all.

"Hades." The voice echoes behind me. A chill runs down my spine as my body is paralyzed.

The voice is three-toned. I know it at once, but the anger cannot be tamed for me to return attention to them.

I destroy another soul. It fights, digging its nails into my skin, forcing blood to spill, but I hardly feel it.

I ignore the ferocity in the soul's eyes and pull until it comes apart with a last, dying scream.

Out of the corner of my eye, I can see them. The Fates. Standing there in the gowns that shift and change. Their clothes seem to match, then shift again. Part of their trick. They are of the past and the future. They are of the present. They are of fate and prophecy, and yet they have given me this.

I sacrificed my life for all. To be condemned here within the confines of the Underworld. Alone and yet surrounded by all.

The only thing that matters to me is gone. My soulmate. My love. My queen. My everything.

This is how Zeus wanted it. How the Fates allowed it.

He wanted me to rage and suffer and despair. I know that I am playing into his hands by feeling these things, by acting on them, but I cannot stop. The pain is too great.

He will pay. They will all pay.

"Hades," the Fates cry out again, their tone demanding this time. I do not look at them although my body stills. I reach for another soul and destroy it without registering any of its features. This soul barely had any fight left. Perhaps it had been tortured enough.

"You act as if Persephone is gone forever."

"She very well might be," I spit in the direction of the Fates. I cannot make out their features clearly, but I can see that they judge me. That they find me lacking.

As losing my mind. As *evil*. "There must have been a way where she did not need to leave."

There must've been, the thought hisses in the back of my mind.

There is silence. Nothing but silence between us.

I turn away and reach for another soul. This one is strong and determined and tries to wrench itself out of my grasp. I will not let it go. I dig my fingers in and pull with all my strength and all my wrath. It splits with an anguished howl.

A small, quiet part of me points out that it is my anguish the soul has died for. That what I feel is heartbreak, not a thirst for blood.

I do not listen. I cannot listen. What else do I have, if not the power of death after life? *What else do I have?*

Nothing.

"You gain the attention of war," the Fates say, stepping closer. It is a brave thing to do when my hands are not my own. When my strength is not my own. When my only wish is to *destroy*, so that the realms around me can be as broken as I feel. I do not dare to look at a peaceful scene. I do not want to look at things that are *whole* and *untouched*. I want my vision to reflect the carnage inside me.

"Hades," they warn, "the attention of war," they repeat.

I'm always gaining the attention of some entity that wants to torture me. And yet I have always taken it in my stride. I cannot *hide*. I have never been able to hide.

I could not even hide from Persephone, who saw me. And touched me. And let me love her.

And walked away.

She *had* to walk away. I know that. No matter how many times I remind myself that I *know*, it does not help.

Not tonight. Not when my heart has been torn from my chest just as surely as I tear these souls apart. I did not know my heart could be shredded like this.

"Demeter has not stopped," the Fates say.

I whirl around, breathing hard, and force myself to focus on them. They stand by the banks of the river, and suddenly I cannot bear the sight.

I find *myself* standing in the shallow water, chill seeping into my feet.

While the Fates watch, I slosh out of the river and leave.

I am not aware of traveling along the path, nor am I aware of descending into the caverns where souls are punished. I only come back to myself when I find a screaming, bloodied soul and split him into ragged pieces.

When I look up from my work, the Fates are watching, expressions impassive.

"She has not stopped," they repeat.

"I know that!" My head aches. A mother's pain is brutal, and I feel it etched in the souls I hold in my hands. It is my doing. I need more to ruin. I need more to destroy. I need more to *end*, since I cannot end myself."I *know*. The souls are Demeter's doing." I gesture to the remains at my feet. "And this is mine. Do you have a point? I am growing tired of waiting to reach it."

"You wish for war. We have warned you, Hades. Zeus will win."

"I wish for *Persephone*," I growl, and then I cannot stop. "If war is what must happen, I will meet it. I will not live without her."

A scream of pure fury, pure rage shakes my teeth. My throat cannot possibly sustain it, but it does. My anger is too deep, too raw, never-ending. Until she is back in my arms.

Zeus will not win. And if he *wins*, as the Fates seem to think he will, then it will be an empty victory, because there will be nothing left for him to claim.

I move through the cavern like a whirlwind, destroying every soul that crosses my path. There is not enough blood in all the Underworld to satisfy me. There is certainly not enough in these caverns, so when I find myself at an exit, I leave.

But I will not stop. I cannot stop. Every time my mind grasps for calm, a memory of Persephone resurfaces. Persephone, ill and afraid on the rug in my rooms. Persephone, sated and pleasured in my bed. Persephone, beside me at court, looking upon the souls to be judged with empathy and care.

Persephone, looking back at me as she left. *As she left me.*

Regret is a horrid thing.

These memories are so painful in her absence that

others force their way into my mind. I do not want to think of my years of torturous isolation, but each one of them plays out in my thoughts. The hopelessness. The dark. The knowledge that I would never be free.

No one gave me mercy. No one could understand. I didn't know that what I needed was love until I had it and then lost it.

Before her, nothing mattered. There was no one to miss me. No one to wait for my return home. No one to love me.

No one to touch me.

There is no one here to touch me anymore. Not the way she did.

I rage through the Underworld, screaming her name, ripping and tearing. Biting and clawing. Destroying and destroying and destroying. Hundreds of souls. Multitudes.

I cover the entire Underworld in a layer of ash.

I have been burned to the ground. Imbalance is what Demeter wanted, and I will level it all, death will be her legacy as well. Unless Persephone returns to me, all that will exist is death. So mote it be.

chapter 3

MY FATHER'S FACE TWISTS AS MY WORDS sink in. The confession of the seeds, the taste of which still linger on my lips. His mouth curls downward, and the rest of his expression follows suit—

But only for a split second.

He manages to change it to confusion, his eyes going wide. My father shakes his head, as if in disbelief.

Is he going to make me repeat what I just said? I ate the seeds.

I will if he requires. What is done is done and I will face the consequences. Whatever that may be.

My mind drifts to my mother in the silence that follows. The pastures have withered here, a sign that my mother has gone. The muted browns of the field surrounding the towers are pitiful. Death surrounds us.

I don't dare test my magic, not while so many eyes lay on us. But my fingers twitch with the need to bring life back to these halls.

And the need to see my mother. Would she gaze upon me with horror and shock as my father's just done.

All over the seeds.

Because of the pomegranates? My heart races, remembering Hades's plea and Hecate's reaction. As if she's aware of my thoughts shifting to her, Hecate disappears from behind me. I do not watch her, but I feel her go. There is an absence in the air, and a slight wind rushes through the hall. My father's eyes lift from my face, then drop back down.

If he does not speak soon, I will have to continue. I will have to say *something*. Because more questions are coming into my mind. They are growing like weeds. The only way to pluck them out is to find answers.

"Father," I begin, but the doors of the main hall slam open with a loud bang. Hastened steps of my mother and her companions fill the room.

"Persephone!" Her tone is strained with desperation. Although she says my name as if it is a prayer.

I turn toward my mother's voice, my heart swelling, my father's hands slipping away from me as I do. His fingers brush my back.

My mother.

With a dry throat, I rush forward a few steps, but my mother is already running. She sprints across the shining floor, the skirt of her flowing black dress flying behind her and her arms stretched out to me.

She's abandoned her green dress for black, for mourning and death.

I barely have time for another step before I collide with her. My mother's hair falls all around me, tickling my face as she closes her arms tight around my body. We're so close that I can feel her pounding heart and her fast, unsteady breath.

Tears prick from the relief of being beside her. My mother. I've missed her so much. I'd speak but I don't trust my voice. My throat is tight and dry, and my body refuses to do anything but cling to my mother.

"Persephone," she says into my hair, her voice trembling. "My daughter. *Persephone.*" Her voice is strong and yet gentle. A warm tear falls from her cheek to mine.

Mother. I'm so sorry. I'm so sorry.

The relief in her voice makes my heart twist. I have missed her *so* much. I know that her love for me is genuine. There is no hidden meaning in her words, she's not careful about her emotions the way my father is when he speaks.

I couldn't hold her any closer if I wanted to. The two of us embrace as if unsure if we would see each other again. Because that's the harshest truth. That moment existed, that memory and nightmare wove itself in our days and nights that are behind us.

Never again do I wish to mourn that loss. Never. She is my mother and I love her dearly.

"I missed you," I whisper into her hair as my own tears fall. The scent of her, the warmth of her. The comfort of being in her embrace is exactly what I needed to breathe here in this hall.

I have worried after her. I have wanted to reassure her, and be reassured, too. I wanted her to stroke my hair and tell me it would be all right. Tell me she understood.

She doesn't say a thing to me, but they are all communicated in her touch.

Only…

I know, too, that it may not be all right. That something is not right. That Hecate and Hades have an understanding that somehow involved bringing me to Olympus. That my mother is involved. I wish I could take it all back. There's been so much destruction and death.

My mind scrambles to create a way where every wrong is righted. My mother, from how she refuses to let go and how she is breathing into my hair, her breaths hitching like she may be crying, is beside herself.

The gods have created an imbalance. Your mother—

Was Hades right? Did my mother really do this? For me?

She's never been one for violence. Never wanted harm to come to anyone. She's the most generous of the gods. And yet death and despair follow in her wake.

I've never known such things, but I've also never known grief like I did losing her. I can only imagine how she felt.

I hold her back, breathing slowly and steadily to keep myself calm. Surely there is a way to stop it. To bring life back. To let what happened stay behind us.

Mothers would do unfathomable things for their daughters.

Unfathomable. That is the word Hades used. The souls filling the sky seemed unfathomable to me.

My mother would do no such thing!

I can feel in her touch that she would. That she might do worse, if she thought it would bring me back to her.

The imbalances.

All the deaths.

The souls in the sky above the Underworld. The destruction of our realms.

Hades. My mind stays on thoughts of him as I stare at my mother.

I stroke my mother's back in rhythmic circles. She relaxes into me, and I realize I'm frowning into the distance.

I let my face rest on her shoulder, hiding it from anyone who may be watching. Olympus feels strange, but my mother does not. I keep holding her, nearly afraid of letting her go.

And I need a few more seconds to think.

Is there something I can say, here and now, that will ease tensions created?

I cannot say I wish to go back to the Underworld. They will not understand. Nor is there a way. The realms are closed. Hades never had a right to take me as he did.

The anger I imagine my mother will feel at the mention of his name…

My heart aches. A wretched pain as my throat closes once again. I need both of them. My mother and this beautiful life that surrounds me, and Hades, the other half of my soul and the realm I'm rightfully queen of.

How…how can it be so? From the corner of my eyes, tears form and take far too long to fall as I attempt to hide my thoughts from prying eyes.

Behind me, my father, the king of the gods, clears his throat. "Demeter…" His tone is comforting and yet demanding.

My mother squeezes me tighter, whispering something I can't hear into my hair. It's too rushed and spoken too quietly. Then she straightens. "We are going."

"Demeter," my father says, irritation sharpening his tone. "Persephone has—"

"Whatever it is can surely wait!" my mother cries. I blink. It's not like her to raise her voice in the main hall. My body tenses. That's when I get a good look at her. Her eyes are red-rimmed and her expression hollow. As if she has not slept in ages. Her bottom lip wobbles slightly as she tells Zeus, "I insist that it wait. I need time with my daughter."

For a moment, I think my father will refuse. I imagine he will demand that we stay with him in the main hall or one of the more private rooms nearby. I don't know what there is for him to say about the pomegranate seeds, but I can't imagine there is any way he can change it.

Gods have many powers, but I have never known my father to be able to make someone un-eat pomegranate seeds. I'm aware it must've bound me to Hades in some way. Or protected me.

Power and magic do not work the same way in every realm. Things that may be undone with magic or powers in one realm are permanent in others. At that moment when Hades handed me the seeds, I had to accept them. It was all I knew of comfort to do as he wished.

The moment passes. My father huffs, giving up, and my mother takes my hand, squeezing tightly. He concedes, granting her wish.

Voices rise all around us as she guides me out of the main hall with haste. The crowd parts for us and I dare not look any of them in the eye. I know not which gods came to watch. With everything that has happened, I am more lost than anything, and one place that is always home is in my mother's arms.

Before I went to the Underworld, I would have fretted about what the crowd in the courts saw and what they thought. I would have wondered for hours whether anyone had noticed that I had changed. I thought it would be my life's greatest failure and disaster if anyone but Beatrice was to learn that my powers were slipping away.

And now it is clear that they know so very little that I cannot expend a thought on what they may think of me and of what happened. They cannot possibly know the love that binds Hades and me.

My mother walks quickly down one hall, then another, then stops and hugs me again. She takes several deep breaths although her hand still trembles. I know she is trying to calm herself. Remind herself that I am still here. Then she pulls away, and we keep walking hand in hand until we reach my rooms.

The torches light our way down the carved marble steps and all the while I avoid the eyes of servants in the same manner that I avoid staring at the withered plants along the way.

They've all died.

A quick glance around as we enter tells me that it has been tidied. The stone is in its place on my altar. There is no sign of someone stealing in to take me away.

As my eyes land on the ground where I last sat, a chill comes over me. The fear in the memory has not left me.

"It's alright," my mother whispers and holds me tightly as if she knows the terror I felt. "No one will ever take you away again."

I do not know what I expected. Torn bedding, perhaps? Scratches on the floor? There wouldn't be any. I did not fight. I did not know anyone had come to retrieve me. It became very dark and very cold, and I sank into it like a person might sink into a frigid lake.

My mother closes the doors behind us and comes to me, taking my face in her small hands. They're cold to the touch at first, but quickly warm. Her eyes are filled with worry.

I'm filled with worry, too. I put my hands over hers and gaze into her beautiful green eyes. The things Hades said and the things I have witnessed come together.

"Mother," I say softly. "Did you go to the mortal realm?" It's almost a whisper. I don't want it to be true.

Her eyes narrow, and tears glisten in the corners. Again her bottom lip wavers. They are *angry* tears. Her anger does not look like my father's.

"You were gone." Her voice nearly cracks under the emotion. "You had been taken from me, and I could not find you." She swallows thickly. "Worst of all, they knew where you were and didn't tell me. I know it in my heart." Her words hit with a vengeance.

"Who—" I try to start but she hushes me. Who could have known where I was? I don't understand what she's thinking.

"I will not let that go unpunished," my mother continues. "The way I have suffered must be repaid, and it has not been. The realms owe me. They owe *you*. They will feel it all. Every bit of agony I felt."

"Mother." I breathe, pressing my hands more firmly into hers. I will not pull away from her. I will *not*. She is my mother, and I love her, and I *feel* her pain. I feel the tears in her eyes as if they are my own. But the things she has done—that Hades *told* me she did but I refused to believe—these things are unfathomable. "This is not *you*."

"It is me," she argues, a tear slipping out of her eye and dripping down her cheek. Her face is pink. Her upset is palpable, and I *understand* it. That may be the worst part. I understand, because I feel it as well, how she missed me. I was desperate for her, too. "Grief is for us all."

"Destruction is *not*. Mother, you must see that. It is not the fault of the mortals—"

"It is not as if Hades would care about what *I* felt. What his selfishness caused. He only cares about his realm. He could never have anticipated how much I care for my daughter." Her eyes go soft, and her lips tremble. "Oh, Persephone."

My eyes search hers for what she knows. Does she know he loves me? Does she know I love him as well? My words refuse to leave my lips, caught in my throat. What will she do if I tell her how I've fallen for the god of the Underworld.

"I will not say a word against your anger," I murmur, looking into her eyes. For the first time on Olympus, I feel…I must stand on my own. I know what I believe, and I know it is wrong to punish mortals for the actions of gods. It has been done before—*many* times—but that does not mean it is right. This is not my mother. She doesn't wish for suffering. "But you have heard their prayers. You have been there for mortals. Helped them with their harvest. Gave them comfort. They are *your* people. What happened was not their fault."

My mother lets out a long exhale and wipes away a few more tears with the sleeve of her gown.

"You have always been like this, haven't you?" With

a little laugh, she brings her hand to my face. "You have never loved your shadow side."

"My *shadow* side—"

"But I have been forced to make peace with mine," she says over me. "It is not my fault, either, Persephone. Having you taken to the Underworld"—her hands shake—"that would *never* be my doing. Never."

That sends another wave of fear through my body. No—of course she would not have allowed me to be taken to the Underworld.

And if I had never gone…

Would I have learned about magic from someone like Beatrice? Would I have spent my days wandering the paths of the realm, greeting others without thoughts of myself?

Would I know what it is to sit next to Hades at court and look upon the souls who had passed into his realm? To show mercy in ways he cannot.

No. Of course I would not have. And something inside me says I *needed* those experiences. I needed them more than I ever could have known. Again my fingers twitch with the need for magic and power to come to life. But I grip my hands together, not wanting to test it here.

I don't know what to say to my mother. Her expression is still filled with agony. Her hand refuses to let me go. Perhaps she needs only time to see reason.

"I missed you," I say. "I missed you so much. I know this is not the only side of you. Please…I am not harmed. I am not ill. I am… Mother, I am doing very well."

Her eyes flicker all over my face, and a crease appears in her forehead. "Are you?" Pain is etched into her expression. Concern riddled in her gaze.

"Yes! I promise! I give you my word. I am *well*. I am—" There are no words to describe what Hades has done for me. Not in terms my mother will understand. "I am well," I say again, stepping closer. "Please know that I am well. There is nothing to avenge."

My mother smiles, her eyes still shining with tears. She makes a sound that is not really agreement. My mother still thinks there *is* something to avenge.

She might even think I am lying to her. Hiding some pain from her.

My mother takes a half-step back and smooths down my hair again. She curls a lock gently around her finger and hooks it behind my ear, then squeezes my hands, dropping them only after a long moment.

"Come with me, Persephone. Let me hold you. I have missed you so much."

With my hands in hers, I allow us this moment, and I try to silence the memory of the screams of thousands of souls tortured in the Underworld at the hands of my mother.

chapter 4

Hades

HOW MUCH TIME MUST PASS? BEFORE SHE IS *returned or before I snap?*

"My Lord," Minox says. His voice is dull. Distant. Barely louder than a whisper. It cannot be louder than the breeze in my mind. His voice is cloaked in darkness as he is.

I'm aware it's not real, but the image before me is vivid.

Persephone, standing in the meadow. The sun shines down on her hair. She bends to pick a flower and twirls it in her fingers, then brings it to her nose to inhale its scent. Her beauty and grace are unmatched. The depths of my soul long to be beside her, but that reality will never be. I can never leave the Underworld. She must return to me. *She must.*

In my vision, the breeze moves through the trees.

There are footsteps nearby. Creatures of the forest, perhaps. Inhabitants of the Underworld. I do not know, and I do not care. I cannot take my eyes off her.

Persephone lifts her head from the flower, and her face brightens. The fog rolls in between the rows and rows of florals. The faint purple hues mixed with the fog only add to her ethereal beauty. The smile across her face cannot be for me—for I've taken that life from her—but after a moment, she lifts her hand and waves to me. Her delicate features are calling to me.

Her lips form my name, but no sound reaches me. Perhaps I'm meant to build her the castle in the foreground, to ensure she has the florals she's always wanted and needed. For the death here will not do. Maybe in a liminal space. Somewhere between the Underworld and Olympus. Somewhere we can run away together for a moment. Just to hold her. To have her warmth in my embrace. Hecate…could she make such a reality possible?

"My Lord," Minox says again, a touch louder this time. As if he believes I hadn't heard him. I did. I do not care for company or requests at this time. The rage has left me hollow. There's nothing left of me to offer.

"No," I answer.

I cannot seem to get closer to Persephone, but it is all I can think of. I need to know if she's safe. I need to touch her. The skirts of her gown blow gently in the breeze, the fabric ripping in the air. Is she happy? Does she find joy in these moments where I find pain?

She's beautiful in the summer. Gorgeous. There is no

comparison. It's Persephone who gives the meadow its beauty. It's Persephone who makes the sun shine.

I used to dream about the sun. I used to dream about the light.

In those centuries that I was trapped in that dark pit, I wished for the light. Even a single beam would do. There is no doubt I could offer Hecate something she's always wanted. The power that exists here behind the walls of the Underworld… If only she could offer a safe haven for the two of us. Is it possible?

"My Lord." A hand squeezes my shoulder. It is a gentle touch, but it gets firmer. Minox. It must be him, because it is his voice in my ear, but I do not *want* to speak to him.

The vision of Persephone begins to fade. And in its place the anger returns. The meadow turns gray, then black. Persephone loses color last of all, and I stare at her for as long as I can.

Just one more moment, please.

She is gone.

"Leave me," I seethe. My tone warning as the rage billows in my chest again. Without her presence, I'm only left with the desire to make everything around me feel the pain I feel. Is that not what Demeter did? And she got what she damn well wanted.

"I cannot, my Lord." Minox states and there's a hint of regret in his tone.

I lurch forward in my chair in the lonely bedchambers, my back protesting, and balance my elbows on my knees so I can scrub at my face. My eyes are gritty and my mouth is dry and it occurs to me at this moment that it is possible I have not slept.

How could I fall into a slumber not knowing how she rests.

Minox places a careful hand on my back. The touch hurts as if he has bruised me, but I breathe through the discomfort and do not throw him off. He is too gentle. Too soft with me.

I remind myself of all I know of Minox. I have to clear my throat several times, then swallow. The Fates and Hecate have promised me. I will not negotiate. I merely need patience. I pray I do not lose my sanity while I wait.

"What is it," I rasp at him, rubbing at my face again. This is my kingdom, I must act as a king. For that is what my queen deserves when she returns.

"Zeus has requested a meeting."

Every inch of my body turns to stone. I can barely breathe, and Zeus wants a meeting. My lungs freeze as hatred rips its way through my being.

"Has he?" I say, the question ending with a sound that is nothing like a laugh.

"Yes." Minox answers. "He has offered to meet via scrying."

"Convenient." I lean back in my chair again, tip my head back, and close my eyes.

How long have I been sitting in this chair?

Hours, I think.

I cannot remember coming to my rooms. Last night, I gorged myself on violence and destruction. There will be a record, somewhere, of how many souls I destroyed, but I cannot guess the number. For all I saw was red and then darkness.

Opening my eyes, I glance down at my lap.

My clothes are covered in ash. That, I remember. I wreaked such havoc on the Underworld that it rained ash throughout the realm.

The anger flickers to life again like an ember in the grate.

It is smaller now, or I have depleted myself enough to find some semblance of calm. My arms ache. My hands are calloused and sore.

Minox stands silently at my side, waiting for me to gather myself, his robe is obscenely still as he stands. Not daring to give away that he may breathe. Cerberus sleeps at my feet, snoring. I reach down and pet each of his heads. He did not come after me last night, and I am grateful of that.

"When?" I ask finally. I know not what to say to Zeus given his power in this situation seems to be limited. It is Demeter who wages war. Demeter who has won. And Demeter who wishes for me to suffer still. The little birds have said as much. Although their sightings of Persephone are limited, Demeter has made her wishes known.

Zeus has Persephone. She's on Olympus. She is *with him*, so if he wants a meeting, I have no choice but to take it. I am too hungry for information. I am starved for it, and it has only been one night.

"At your convenience," Minox answers smoothly.

I scoff and heave myself out of the chair. It's not meant for sleeping or for having visions of my queen. My feet ache underneath me. My clothes fit strangely on my body, as if they suffered under my rage.

"That's not what he means, and you know it," I tell Minox. "He means to meet within the hour."

Minox smirks. He looks drawn as well. I do not know how long he has stood guard in this room, waiting for me to wake up—or toss myself out of my vision. I cannot have slept. I do not feel restored.

I doubt I will feel restored until Persephone is back. How can I feel life within me when the very goddess of life has been ripped from me?

"Zeus is not a man known for his patience," he says. "When should I communicate that you will be ready?"

Another flare of anger. I want to keep Zeus waiting. I want to show him how very little I think of him. I want to crush him under my foot. God of the gods. It is what he is supposed to be and he made a promise. I swallow thickly, knowing Demeter's hold on Persephone. Knowing the promise Zeus made and what it required of me. The simmering anger dulls as guilt overwhelms me.

But Persephone is with him, and the longer I toy with him, the longer I feel self-pity…the longer it will be until I have news of her.

"An hour," I say to Minox. "I will meet with him in an hour. We will scry."

An hour is too short a time. Bathing and dressing are both slow and painful, but I push myself through it. The agony exists because I have no control over how she returns to me...or if she does at all.

How quickly I got used to her presence here. How quickly I came to love her.

I brace my hand against the wall and breathe through my clenched teeth for quite some time. My fear is that she will not come back to me. I remember the seeds.

Then I haul myself up again and leave for my andron.

Cerberus is awake. He stretches and pads after me, keeping me company as I walk along the garden path. Crushed obsidian crunches under my boots, just as it has every other time I have made this journey.

It is impossible to make it now without thinking of another conversation I had with Zeus.

That was the day I ordered Minox to bring Persephone to me.

That was the night everything began.

I knew some things would change when Persephone came to the Underworld. I did not know she would shift my being so entirely. That she would control this much of me. I knew not how devastating love was to have and then lose.

I didn't know I would fall for her with such depth. I didn't know I would come to need her more than I have ever needed anything.

When I was trapped in the dark, I didn't need the light as much as I need Persephone now.

I thought I would possess her. I didn't realize how much she would possess all of me in return.

It's deathly quiet as I stalk toward the andron, as gleaming and black as ever, and it is as empty as it was during that meeting with Zeus. My boots click on the floor. The cold air draws close to me as I cross the opulent space, getting closer to the mirror with every step.

My dead heart ticks in my chest with a heaviness that seems to beat from the crown of my head to the bottom of my soles.

I'm torn between the need to hear about my queen and the need to spit in Zeus's face. I would rather smash the mirror into a thousand pieces than speak to him. The war still wages and it is on him to end it.

I wave a hand at the enormous grate in the wall, calling the flames for light. Fire in the grate reminds me of Persephone's sweet body in the firelight. Her image flashes before me.

I stop a few paces away from the mirror, bow my head, and gather as much self-restraint as I can summon.

The glass is dark, obscuring my reflection, but when I step closer, the black shimmer swirls away. The glass becomes glass, surrounded by the familiar herringbone pattern. The back of my teeth clench as I prepare to see

Zeus, the god of the sky, of weather, the god of gods, and the god who betrayed me.

Slowly, the mirror reveals the white walls of Olympus. The brilliant white has returned unlike Zeus himself.

His throne is vacant as I stare at it—another one of his games. No matter how long I keep him waiting, he will always keep me waiting a little longer.

Irritation pricks at the back of my neck.

The Underworld is ruined for me already. Nothing the Fates had to say about the situation made it any less bitter.

Zeus steps in front of the mirror, his back straight and his chin up, and sits on the throne. He adjusts his white cloak and as he does, the gold wreath of olive leaves stays firm on his crown. His gaze reaches mine as he sits regally, and the light in his eyes makes me want to strangle him.

His perfection is an insult.

"Hades," he says, and tips his head as if he's found me here by accident. Some bullshit happy coincidence. "I'm glad you could find the time to speak to me."

My voice is gravelly and low in return. He must know of my suffering, so I don't attempt to hide it. "What is it you want?"

He blinks, his eyebrows going up a fraction. "Has something happened? You don't seem like yourself."

My eyes narrow with pure hatred as I stare at him

in the mirror. "Why don't you tell me? Minox made it seem as if your request was urgent."

Zeus spares me useless comments and clears his throat instead.

"Hecate has returned Persephone to Olympus," he announces, his expression neutral. At least, it is meant to be neutral. It does not hide anything from me. Zeus didn't want Persephone to return. He wanted her to be mortal and to dwell in the Underworld as a soul. Her power was to never threaten his. That way, the prophecy could not come true. She would not surpass him as it was foretold one of his offspring would. It was a tit for tat. I was to be given my queen, and he was to have a threat removed from his castle in the sky.

I suppose we both betrayed one another. I wanted my queen in her power, not for the life to be taken from her only so that I may possess a shell of the goddess she was.

"You're aware she's returned safely, yes?"

"Yes," I say, after a beat. "I am aware."

He waits.

I wait. The seconds burn between us. Questions collide in my mind, but my throat is too tight to speak them.

I let my gaze wander in the mirror, studying the blue accents on the walls behind Zeus and preparing some things to say if he insists on having this discussion for much longer. We both know Demeter has been on a rampage. We both know there are too many souls coming to the Underworld.

We both know that it is Demeter who must be convinced to see reason, not me.

"Demeter has not stopped—"

"You've gone too far," Zeus says, leaning toward the mirror. One side of his mouth turns down.

It is difficult—almost impossible—to be in this room and to look at his face, even separated as we are by the mirror. I make my eyes wider to give the impression of mild surprise.

"Have I?"

Zeus narrows his eyes. The side of his jaw ticks, but he forces his teeth apart and takes a breath. "You know you have, Hades."

I watch him in the mirror for a long moment, then hold my hand out in front of me and study my hands. I took out my anger on the Underworld with my bare hands, and they tell the tale with blood still dried under my nails.

The mortal souls have paid the price as well.

Zeus shifts in his throne. He's never cared much for seeming to be impatient. He doesn't like to let others know when they have gotten under his skin.

It is no use with me. I know he is frustrated. I can feel it through the mirror.

"I believe I followed the terms of our agreement," I state. "She was to rule beside me as queen, and she is more than prepared to do so."

"You gave her pomegranate seeds. She *ate* them."

A smirk lifts my lips up half-heartedly. Hope

returning. "Well, yes. Persephone is to be returned to me, so I offered her the pomegranate. All know of what it means to consume the seeds of the Underworld."

"So you decided to guarantee it for yourself?"

"It was already guaranteed. Wasn't it?" I ask smoothly, my voice level but my heart racing.

Zeus scowls at me. "That act was not part of the terms."

"Of course it was. It was implied. You knew that when you arranged for her to be sent to me."

He looks off to the side and swallows, the cords in his throat tightening. His vulnerability is…curious. *What's his aim?* These are the things *he* wanted. These are the terms *he* agreed to. It's true that Demeter's rage was far stronger than expected, but it is not a reason to violate the laws of the gods.

There are consequences for breaking those rules, even for a god as powerful as Zeus.

I will see to it that he faces them if he has come to tell me he's changed his mind. Fear causes my heart to race. He cannot. He will not.

"Hades," he begins, and I know that tone. It is far too light for the tension in his face and the anger in his eyes. This has not played out the way he wanted. It has not gone according to whatever plan he thought would benefit him the most. Now he will be looking for an escape. Some bargain he can make to free him from the terms between us. "You must see how…tenuous the situation has become. You must see—"

"I must see Persephone."

Zeus sighs. "That is not what I—"

"I wish to see her, to see my queen," I press, though I do not allow my voice to rise. I keep my words calm, almost flat, so that Zeus will know I am not here to be baited. I'm here to tell him what he can give me. Only a moment. I need to see her. To speak with her. Desperation is unbecoming but if it's what it takes, I'll allow it.

"That is not possible," says Zeus. "I cannot let her return to the Underworld."

I give him a look. "You do not come to the Underworld to speak to me. Persephone does not need to do that, either. Let me speak to her." I swallow thickly, knowing the depths of what I ask. "Allow her the scry of Olympus."

chapter 5

Persephone

THE CROSSROADS SCRY IS FOR THE GOD OF gods. It's for my father. For gods with needs and rights to speak with those in liminal spaces and on the other side of the crossroads.

For Hecate. For Hades.

Not for me, but the very thought of Hades, my lover, wanting me? My throat is tight with need to speak to him, and I'm drawn in like a moth to the flame. My heart pains and it hurts me in a way that was there before I knew I'd get to speak to him and yet could not give it attention because the pain is too much to bear.

I need him. My Hades. My king. If for no other reason than to know he still wants me and feels the same as I do.

My gaze is caught by a small figurine made of both copper and silver. It's a bud and the petals pull back and part allowing a small trinket to be placed inside. Long ago when I was only a child, a mortal witch blessed it to play music when opened as an offering to my mother. She wanted a child of her own and my mother so willingly provided one before the woman could even ask. My mother bestowed the gift upon me, telling me of the greatness it is to be a goddess. To be loved and needed.

All of my life, I saw it as a blessing—until the days my powers withered and then it was a curse. A daily reminder of what I was losing. Picking up the small bud I don't dare pull the petal back and hear the song. Not until I've tested my magic.

I wish I could have taken the prized possession with me to the Underworld. Oh how Silvie would have loved it. Not only that but I could have shared it with Hades. I could have told him how I believed for the longest time the small trinket held my magic.

For the witch was powerful and so was my mother. And I held a piece of both of them forever with the musical bud.

Hades doesn't know that side of me. I never thought to tell him. If only I could in this moment while my memory serves me so well. Regrets flare from how we started. So much regret and pain.

Lightning strikes in a vision storm in the distance, the thunder booming immediately after and ripping through the skies so violently it causes my heart to race.

Swallowing thickly, I gather up the courage to ask my

father. The atmosphere is still and tense here. Lighting strikes violently from the sky and I know it's my father's anger. My fingers twist around one another and I hesitate.

Alone in my rooms, I stare at a scry of my own. It cannot reach through crossroads, like the Underworld, and yet, it's how I first saw him. There was a way…chills glide down my arms as if to confirm. He broke the gods' law of realms to see me. Perhaps I don't need my father. Perhaps if I stare long enough, Hades will appear. It's a torturous thing to be subject to my father's will.

The perfectly polished obsidian stares back at me as I'm tucked in a corner of the bed. Staring and wishing, but hopelessly dependent on the wills of others.

I look at myself in the mirror, the morning light shining on perfect glass. And for a moment, I see my mother.

Not Hades, but the memory of my mother from last evening.

We sat together, her arms around me and my head on her shoulder, while she told me over and over how upset she had been. How she missed me like she would miss her own heart. How she would miss the sun or the seasons in the mortal world. Her voice swelled with pain over and over, and her hands would clutch at my hair, then relax again when she realized I was back.

I've never seen my mother so distraught. I know how I longed for her, but I had Hades and my magic to occupy my thoughts. My mother had a hole in her heart and my empty room and no knowledge of what had happened to me or whether I still had breath in my lungs.

I cried with her when she confessed she barely had hope that I was still alive, but hope was there.

I told her I missed her, too. It was the truth. It *is* the truth. I was so afraid, in the Underworld, that I might never see her or speak to her again, and that thought had been unbearable. It made me fold up into myself, scared to move a muscle in case I made those horrible thoughts come true.

I missed her—but I do not like the idea of her causing so much pain in the mortal world. That is the kind of change that speaks of ruin. Her anger is frightening. Her vengeance is brutal. I've never known this side of my mother, but then again, she'd never known loss like she did those days of my absence.

Lightning strikes again and this time I only flinch. The war still rages as Demeter copes with Zeus's betrayal. It seems impossible to calm my mother. To soothe her pain.

I don't know how to explain to my mother that she does not need to be ruined. I wasn't ruined in the Underworld, and I have not been given back to her a broken shell of myself.

If anything, I was a shell of myself before, on Olympus, when my powers were ebbing away and I was staring into a future as a forest nymph.

Eventually, food was brought. Hades's order repeated in my mind again.

Do not drink the wine your father gives you.

I looked at the cask of wine brought by the servants. Would that wine count if it was not given to me by Zeus himself? I did not drink it, choosing water flavored with nectar instead. If my mother noticed, she did not point it out.

We stayed together as the sun set, glowing in through the windows until at last the stars covered the sky. I got into my bed, which felt as strange and new as the rest of Olympus. All the nights I slept here before seem like they were lifetimes ago. Perhaps I did not expect to lay my head here again. Perhaps that is why it took me so long to fall asleep.

My mother sat by the bed until I drifted off. When I woke in the night, she was not here, but she returned in the morning, not long after I woke.

We had tea and light and airy sweet cakes for breakfast. She brought out a gown for me to wear, simple and white, yet beautiful, and I sat at her feet while she braided my hair.

And still she cried, her tears falling on the delicate fabric of my dress. Demeter's sadness is palpable, I feel anguish for my mother.

Now I stand in front of the mirror, looking into the face of a woman I do not know.

I turn my head from side to side, letting my eyes travel over my eyebrows, my nose, my mouth. The braid in my hair, which curls down over my shoulder and meets the clasp of my gown.

My features are the same. I cannot pick out any obvious differences. The slope of my nose and the bow of my lips—the same. The point of my chin—the same. The pink in my cheeks—

It's the same, isn't it? Perhaps, under my eyes is slightly darker from the lack of sleep.

I lean closer. My cheeks are pinker than they were when I left, but then—I had not been well when I arrived in the Underworld. And I had not been well for some time before that. Fear can make a person unwell. It can even make a goddess unwell.

Shouldn't I look unwell?

I don't.

I step back from the mirror and lift my hands to my hair, patting carefully at the braid so I don't disturb my mother's work. Her fingers had been so gentle. So loving. She sewed protection within the braids. Chanting her love and that I am divinely protected, divinely guided, and being shown the best of all the worlds and nothing less.

No matter what happens, I will treasure this, at least. It is a sign of her love for me as my mother, and I cannot be ungrateful for that. Even if I crave a world she'll never know. Even if I could not find the courage to tell her I'd fallen in love with the god she loathes.

I take a deep breath and close my eyes, turning my mind to how I felt when Silvie came to my rooms in the Underworld. I didn't know what to think of her at first. I worried she had been sent to—

I'm not sure. Spy on me, or encourage me to do dangerous things, or control me.

But she did not.

She taught me what she knew of the powers in the Underworld. She guided me through the knowledge I was missing, again and again until I understood it for myself.

It was because of Silvie that I was able to enchant the bells on my door and light fires in the hearth. It was Silvie who gave me the confidence to walk on the path in Hades's realm, speaking to those I met and learning from them, too.

I may be in Olympus, but I will be just as confident here. I will demand my magic. I will demand that my will be heard…but at what cost?

A soft knock at the door brings me out of those memories and back into the light.

"You may enter," I call.

The doors to my chambers open, and Beatrice hurries across the threshold, her skirts in one hand and her eyes wide.

A well of emotion floods me once again. The damned emotions coming and going like a righteous storm commanded by Poseidon himself.

I rush for her and throw my arms around her as the door closes softly behind us. Beatrice embraces me back just as tightly, her face pressed to mine and her hands clutching at my back. Her warmth and relief are evident.

"You are here," she breathes as if in prayer.

"Persephone. You're here. I could hardly believe the news when I heard. I thought—"

"I should have come to you." My heart aches with guilt. "When I arrived…I was not thinking, Beatrice, or I would have come to see you—"

"Are you all right? Are you hurt? What happened? You were gone in the night, and by the time I realized—" Her questions come one after the other, each just as desperate to be answered.

"The Underworld," I whisper. "I was in the Underworld with Hades."

Beatrice pulls back, looking into my eyes with a shocked expression and something else in the depth of her gaze that I cannot place. "It is true, then?"

"Is that what was said? That I had gone to the Underworld?"

"Yes, but…" She lifts one of her hands to cover her mouth, then squeezes me again before she straightens. "I thought it could not be. You are a goddess of Olympus, and—"

"It is true! And I…" I take her hands in mine, wishing I could tell her everything in a single breath while also wishing I did not have to say out loud the truth of how this reality came to be. "I don't know how to describe it to you. It is a realm like—you can only imagine it, Beatrice. It is like the stories, but so much more."

"I've heard the stories, but once you were gone…" She shakes her head, her chest heaving with a deep breath as her expression turns somber. "Once you were gone, Olympus became a hell of its own. Your mother's grief and sorrow clouded the skies. Everyone had their say. So many whispers—"

"But you knew. You thought I had gone to the Underworld. Why?"

"Because there was nowhere else you could be. And…and I had a dream from Hecate… she whispered to have faith and that you were well but trapped. You were not among the mortals. You were not with any of the other gods. You were lost to your mother, and when she realized she could not find you in any of the places she knew and guarded, I prayed and made offerings to the one goddess, the Titan who rules every crossroad… but how? How did you get there?"

I frown, remembering. "Someone *did* take me. Someone…brought me to him."

"Who?"

"I do not know. I do not remember." I remember the cold. I remember the dark, the chill that ran down my spine. But now, with Beatrice's hands in mine, I am certain it could not have been Hades. If he had the power to come to Olympus, he would be here with me now. He would not have let Hecate bring me here without staying at my side.

He *cannot* come to Olympus. It must be beyond his power. Someone did though. Someone broke the law of the gods.

"But *you* did not choose to go?" Beatrice searches my eyes. "There were some who thought you slipped away, intending to disappear. I told them you would never. Tell me I know you well enough to—"

"I would not do that to my mother," I answer solemnly. "Never would have left without telling you either."

"That is what I said!" Beatrice exhales. "That is exactly what I said to anyone who would listen. But it was not my place…"

She squeezes my hands and then releases them quickly, bowing her head slightly, seeming to remember that I am a goddess, and she is a companion. This closeness between us is not our usual habit, even if she knew all my darkest secrets before I went to the Underworld. I grab her hands again. I do not care what our old habits used to be. I'm not my old habits anymore. Beatrice smiles, glancing down at our hands, then brings her gaze back to mine.

"That is what I said," she repeats, quieter this time. "I didn't think it was like you to run away."

"I would not."

Beatrice's expression softens, yet becomes more serious. She presses her lips together. "It was…difficult. While you were gone."

"Tell me please. You have my confidence."

"Your mother was in great distress." She bites her lip for a moment, clearly worried. "Your father was no help at all."

"You can tell me, Beatrice. I've heard some of what happened."

"She took her anger out on first Zeus then Olympus.

When you could not be found, she turned to the mortal world to upset the balance of the gods. She refused to provide life or harvest. Food and plants became scarce. Many have lost their lives. She demanded we all feel her pain and loss. Such a giving god, so gracious and compassionate, turned to wrath and spite."

My eyes slowly close as I do my best to contain the anguish of knowing what my mother is capable of. My mother loves me so much she was willing to cause incredible pain, but I have always known her to treasure the mortals who pray to her. They are a gift. She told me such.

I open my eyes. "And has she given any sign she will stop?"

Beatrice shakes her head. "She has not given the mortal realm relief."

"She must," I murmur, then clear my throat. "I will speak to her. I will do my best to convince her that there must be a reprieve."

"My lady…Persephone," Beatrice says quietly, seeming uncomfortable with the question in her mind. She nearly whispers the question, "Did he hurt you?"

I thought he did. I thought Hades was a monster who had crept up to Olympus and taken me from my bedroom. I thought he made me a prisoner so he could break me down and hurt me for his own enjoyment. It is odd how my recollection has changed. Or rather what I care to admit has changed.

I don't wish to lie to Beatrice. I cannot tell her all

of what Hades did for me, but I won't give her the impression that he harmed me for his own entertainment. He never did, but I cannot say the process of coming to terms with myself was entirely without pain.

"He showed me the parts of myself that feel pain," I say finally, the words finally fitting with the experience, at least enough to share them with Beatrice. "And in doing so, he gave me power over it."

Beatrice studies me again for a long moment, then seems to find honesty in my face and smiles, the corners of her eyes crinkling.

"You look well," she whispers, as if it is supposed to be a secret. "Truly, you are not afraid?"

"I'm not afraid," I confirm and offer her a simper.

She smiles back, her eyes sparkling, and hugs me once again.

After a beat, she releases me and steps back, taking on a more deferent stance, her hands folded in front of her.

We both take a few breaths, calming down from the rush of our reunion. I cannot believe I did not see her last night. My mother required that time, however, and I can only hope that settling my mother's heart will convince her to have mercy on the mortal realm.

"I am not only here to greet you," Beatrice says and straightens her shoulders. She swallows thickly, "I have come to bring you a message, my queen."

chapter 6

Hades

MY ANDRON GROWS WARM AS THE HOUR I am to speak to Persephone approaches.

I've done my best to keep busy. I've walked my realms for hours. I've taken Cerberus with me, and we have gone to every place I can think of. I've repaired as much damage as I could hunt down, my throat closed with guilt.

It is only the thought of her that provides me with such calmness and intent for justice and balance. Even as the screams of the dead continue to pour through my realm and disrupt what little peace the four corners of the Underworld held.

I'm the cause of much of the damage, but it is not only my doing. It is Demeter's as well. Hecate's.

Zeus's. The righteous anger is barely tamed within me. Like a dog tethered to a collar, I maintain the semblance of control knowing I may see her soon. I must have my Persephone, my queen, my love, my life.

And I cannot promise, even to myself, that I will not cause more damage to my realms. I'm not myself without Persephone. She has changed me. My love for her feels more desperate, and more volatile, than it ever has. To know such loss is a torture that should be saved for the worst of the dead.

Zeus begrudgingly agreed to give Persephone the scry of Olympus. As I understand it, he suffers the wrath of Demeter still. The god of gods has betrayed Demeter, and she's sure of it. But I've agreed to keep what's been between us secret so long as he agrees to uphold the law of the gods. She's eaten the forbidden fruit, I'm sure of it. She will be returned. She must. It is only time that keeps us apart. Unless he makes a very ill-advised decision, I'll speak to her soon.

The wait feels longer than the years I spent alone, hopeless, on the edge of madness.

I lit the fires an hour ago, when I could no longer keep myself away from the andron, then walked around the large space, lighting the fires in the smaller grates as well. The entire room dances with warm reflections. And in them, the memory of her beauty, her sadness and fright, her delight and power. All of her and all she will become. The fire licks into the perfectly polished obsidian, forcing the reflection to look as if I am standing among the flames.

I wish the sight could comfort me. Cerberus whines

beside me at the thought. His howling pain echoes the emptiness in my chest.

I pace across the room more slowly, breathing deeply to calm myself. Impatience makes my muscles ache, so I stretch my arms above my head as I go, trying to ease the tension from my shoulders. In those eons I spent alone, there was nothing to sense but my own body in the dark, so I became accustomed to focusing deeply on each movement. To keep what little sanity remained in the pits of despair.

I do that now. It is not much more effective at passing the time, but it is something.

I will see her soon. The promise of reunion is far more motivating than any other offer.

I need to know she is well.

Persephone is the only person, god *or* mortal, who is fit to rule beside me.

She is the only soul who is fit to hold my hand.

My queen. My *love*. She is my heart and soul. If she is not returned—

Abruptly, I stop at the far end of the andron. Cerberus pads up behind me, his nails clicking on the obsidian floor, and nudges my leg. I lower my hand to pat his middle head, then the one on the left, then the one on the right.

Cerberus gives a soft, questioning bark, then bounds away, leaving the andron for elsewhere. An open field is his most likely destination. He will spend an hour or two chasing after the creatures of the forest and guarding the gates.

And I will see Persephone. The thought brings a warmth to the chill in my bones.

When Cerberus's barks have become too distant to hear, I take measured steps back to the mirror and gesture for the fire in the largest hearth to burn a little brighter. I need Persephone to be able to see my face. I will not leave it dim, as I do when I speak with Zeus.

I approach the mirror with a pounding heart. What *is* this feeling? It is a strange giddiness. Almost violent, but—not. Powerful. That's what it is. I have a powerful urge to see her.

To kiss her.

To fuck her. To claim her once again and ensure she is mine.

Although I cannot do those things through the mirror, my body responds as if it is possible. I groan deep in my throat at the very thought of having her returned to me.

The glass remains black. I clench my fists, release them, and take one more step forward.

The black disappears in a silent vortex. For a few moments, it is clear, like a mortal mirror. I grit my teeth. If it stays clear, and Zeus denies me this contact—if he denies *Persephone* this moment—my rage will be uncontained.

Just when I think that madness will take over, the

glass ripples, and the white walls of Olympus appear. Thump, thump, thump. My blood pounds in my ears.

I involuntarily suck in a breath and move an inch closer. I will not touch the mirror—I will not—but my hand rises as if I might.

More of the walls appear. White, with blue accents. The arched frame of a trellis. A gauzy curtain blowing in the breeze. And—

Persephone.

She sits in front of the mirror, her face illuminated by firelight just as mine is, dressed in delicate white with gorgeous braids. The sun is going down outside Olympus. A pale blue dusk is filling the window behind her. The glowing stars will be out soon. A sight I only see in the scry.

Her eyes go wide and light with pleasure at the sight of me, looking every bit my beautiful queen and companion. With my throat tight, I long for her. To touch her and know she is well. My heart misses a beat as my hand presses against the scry.

It's not been long at all, and yet I drink the sight of her in, hungry for the smallest changes in her.

She stares back at me, her lips curving in a sensual smile. "Hello, my king."

"My queen," I answer, my voice calmer than I thought it would be. My tone deep and even. "You're scrying."

"I am," she agrees, reaching up to touch the end of her braid, and all at once, she looks young and unsure. It is only a flicker, however. It does not last. Persephone draws herself up and becomes my queen again. "And you…are there, wanting me still?"

I do not hesitate. "Always." Her shoulders fall with what seems like relief. Did she think I would lose my love for her so quickly? So easily? Even centuries of tortures in the darkest and deepest pits of hell could not tear my desire for her away from me.

The weight of her words travels through the mirror and into my heart. Not even the space between Olympus and the Underworld can stop me from feeling it.

You…are there. Inside those three words are all the things Persephone hesitates to say. *Where I cannot touch you. Where I cannot speak freely with you. Where we are apart.*

With a deep breath, I attempt to quell the burn of raving in my chest. The sight of Persephone's face in that flickering light has woken every part of my body. My fingers ache to touch her. To give her pleasure. To make her come. I want my tongue on her. I want to be inside her. I want to lift her over me and hold her hips while she rides me.

I *want* her. I *need* her.

My mouth is dry with how intensely I need to have her. I swallow and find Persephone doing the same.

She looks over one shoulder, then the other, then slips out of her chair to the floor, moving closer to the mirror with a sigh.

"No one will enter," she says softly. "But I do not know—"

"We do not need to speak of private things between us, my queen."

A heat from deep within me burns for her. Nothing else matters. I can barely think of anything but her beauty, her softness, her powerful touch, and everything I wish to do to her decadent curves.

Her brow raises, and her pupils darken with her curiosity. Persephone bites her full bottom lip, her teeth digging in. "If we are not scrying to speak, what else is there for us to do?"

"I've needed to know if you are well," I tell her in the same, soft tone. "I can see you are, but much of you is hidden from me." My cock hardens at the thought of seeing more of her. Of sating her from a distance. I do not know how long it will be until I have her again, but I will make the most of this moment and every vision of her I have.

She nods, solemn yet playful, and the flush on her cheeks deepens. It's made even warmer by the firelight. I love my queen in the firelight, with the shadows tracing the lines of her nose and her brow and the slope of her shoulders.

"What would you like to see?" she questions innocently. "I want to put your mind at ease."

"Everything," I say hoarsely, desperately. "*Everything*."

"Hmm." Persephone folds her legs to the side and reaches for the top of her dress. She pulls it down over her arms, revealing her breasts. Her nipples peaked. Persephone gazes down at them with a sultry look, then leans toward the mirror. "I am well here," she murmurs, slipping a finger around one of her nipples. "Can you see?"

Yes, I mean to answer, but no sound comes from my parted lips.

"Yes," I manage to say finally. "Cup them my love. Touch yourself as I would."

She does, her lips pursed in concentration. The pads of my fingers are on fire. I know how the tender flesh of her nipples would feel if I ran my thumb over them. I know how they would feel if I were to pinch them. I could make her moan. If only I could give her pleasure myself…but this will have to do.

"Pluck one," I order her gently. With as much desire in my tone as I can offer. "Between your thumb and forefinger. I crave to watch you."

"Like this?" she asks softly. Obeying beautifully. So beautifully cum leaks from the tip of my cock.

"Yes," I answer in a dark murmur.

Persephone repeats her motion, then pinches harder, tipping her head back and letting out a sound that is almost a moan.

"Now the other." I reach for a glass of whiskey and find none, then snap my fingers and allow one to appear. The ice clinks as I pick up the libation and enjoy myself fully with a gulp of the sweet liquor.

"Ooh," she says, her voice straining to stay quiet.

"Does it hurt?" I question, pausing the theatrics.

"A bit," she admits. "But—"

"Does it make you wet?"

"Yes," she whispers. She adds, her tone lower, "You always do."

"Do you wish it was me toying with your sweet body instead of your own fingers?"

"Yes," she says, her voice quivering.

"What about my mouth? Do you wish I could put my mouth on those nipples and lick and suck them until you squirm, my queen?"

"Yes." Persephone looks up at me from underneath her thick lashes. Her lips part in a tempting way, then close again. "Yes. I do."

"I can't see enough of you. Take off your gown."

Seductively, she wriggles out of the gown, laying it on the chair behind her. Persephone leans out of view of the mirror, showing me the curve of her ass, and then returns and sits naked before the mirror, waiting for me to speak.

"You said you were wet, my queen. So soon?" I murmur.

"From the moment I saw your face," she says and stops short before finishing, glancing away. A beautiful blush colors her cheeks. Is she only pretending to be shy? The rest of her body is arched proudly toward me, showing off her mouthwatering curves. "When I think of you. Every moment. My body craves you."

"Show me." My voice almost gives out. "Spread your legs and show me, my queen."

Persephone parts her knees. Slowly. Deliberately. I

think we're both holding our breath. I'm certainly holding mine. I keep my eyes on her face until I cannot, not for another moment, then let my gaze trail down over her breasts and her belly and finally between her legs.

My cock is painfully rigid at the sight of my queen. My lover and my divine equal. Her sweet pussy is slightly swollen with her arousal, peeking open to reveal her core. Fuck me. I need her more than I could have known.

For a few moments, I don't have any kind of existence. I'm nothing but my gaze, and it's locked between Persephone's thighs, and whatever remains of my being is blistering with primal need.

I roll the heel of my hand over my shaft and swallow thickly. How I need her. Everything in me needs her and to have her pleasure like I did before.

"Touch yourself," I rasp.

Persephone exhales, her lashes fluttering. "How, my king?" A groan of satisfaction leaves me as my cock leaks precum.

"Your fingers. Your clit. Touch yourself," I reply almost too quickly.

She makes a show of it, brushing them slowly down between her breasts, following the same path as my heated gaze. I watch her skim her fingers over her belly button, then the crease of her thigh, and then finally I watch her find her clit and circle it, teasing herself before she finally presses her middle fingers over it and circles.

The small moan is a sound I'll remember for all of

eternity. Her head falls back onto the chair behind her, but she lifts it up again to look at her own fingers.

How I manage to speak, I don't know. "Does it feel good, my queen?"

"Not—" She shivers, which must mean her touch is more firm and greedy. "Not as good as you feel." Her whisper is a beautiful sin.

I groan out loud. "I want you to put two of your fingers inside yourself."

She nods her understanding and slides her other hand between her legs, her fingers tentative at her opening before pushing in. Persephone stifles a louder moan behind closed lips.

"Beautiful," I praise, and catch myself on the frame of the mirror before I realize I have reached for it. "Take your fingers. Take them in deep."

"Not as deep as you," she breathes, almost a whine. "Not as good as you." My love needs me. Fuck, I need her too.

"Pretend," I order her. "Pretend it's me. Pretend I'm there with you." I stroke myself with more vigor. "Faster, my queen. Harder. Do not hold yourself back."

I need this, I almost say but hold myself back. I'm too entranced by how she works her hips into her own fingers, her eyes closed. This is what she looks like when she thinks of me. This is what my queen looks like when she must take her pleasures in my absence.

I hate it, and yet I am proud of her. Proud that she can feel so deeply. Proud that she can take such joy in her own body. The duality is torture only because I have no choice in the matter.

Persephone makes a small feminine groan of pleasure, her fingers moving faster, and then she tenses, her body arching as she comes with a low cry. She closes her mouth and rides out her orgasm, pushing her face into the chair's cushion to hide her sounds.

It's more than pleasure surrounding her. It's power. I can feel it through the mirror. The fires in my andron flare brighter, as if they can sense her power, too. She is every bit a goddess in her divine pleasure.

When she's finished, she falls limp onto the throne, panting, and drags her fingers slowly away from her pussy.

Then she peeks out of the corner of her eye and lifts her slick fingers to her mouth. Oh fuck me.

I watch, wordless, as she sucks her arousal off her fingers, her gorgeous eyes locked on mine. I wish nothing more than to grab her wrist and lick her fingers myself. Mine. She is mine.

It's only when her gaze falls to my cock that I realize I've paused my own movements. Although I'm harder than I can ever remember and in dire need. In need of her. My queen who escapes my touch.

Persephone watches me with something like concern in her eyes.

"What about you, my king?" she questions, her tone gentle.

"I—" I clear my throat again. I need Persephone to

return to me. I need this torture to be over. "I don't think it is wise to linger too long, when scrying. No one else should see you like this."

She nods although the look in her eyes doesn't change. "Are you—"

"I am fine," I answer. "I will be better when you return. I will have my pleasure then."

Persephone quickly turns her head. *Has she heard some sound? A warning that someone is coming.*

"Do not drink from what your father offers," I say, and Persephone looks back at me.

"You have said that about the wine, and I have listened. But why?"

"I cannot speak of what I know. Not here. Do as I wish, my queen."

"I will," Persephone promises, and then the mirror goes dark again.

chapter 7

WITH BATED BREATH I WATCH THE DOOR as the black glass stares back at me. The footsteps I heard in the hall grow fainter. It's not someone coming to speak to me, then.

I stand on shaky legs and sink into the chair, a cream woven blanket tight around me. The fire blazes hot. I'm faintly covered in a fine sheen of sweat, but it's more from my orgasm than the heat of the fire. It's more from seeing Hades than *any* fire.

I close my eyes for a few moments, thinking of him. The relief of seeing him and even pleasing him in that way is immense.

I drank in the sight of his face.

The difference in how I felt about the god prior to being with him and now is like night and day. He didn't look as he did when I met him in the Underworld. He'd seemed cold, then. Cold and powerful and almost unfeeling. It's apparent Hades tried not to show his feelings as we were scrying, but I saw them on his face. The smallest muscles betrayed that he's unhappy about this arrangement. His desire for me is evident. And I love it.

He misses me. I miss him as well.

My heart beat faster as I touched myself. The act felt illicit, like I wasn't supposed to enjoy my own body, and certainly not in front of the king of the Underworld during the act of scrying. It was sexy and passionate. Forbidden and heated. My heart sped up from the sensation, and of course from thinking about the way he touched me when we were in bed. I needed every second of that moment with him. I need it again as soon as it can be granted.

Now that I have had a few moments to collect myself, I know that my heart is not only racing from the pleasure. It is racing because…I'm concerned about Hades. As the high calms and my breathing levels, I know that to be fact.

There's something in his expression that spoke of pain. His dark gaze and low tone give him away. As if it's hurt him deeply to be apart from me. As if it's not a separation he can bear for very long. We are gods. We are king and queen. Surely, we will sustain and continue to rule. My choice was made for the greater good. War is not something I wish to come.

So much death. The gods have caused an imbalance.

He's already told me what it would look like if my

mother doesn't stop, but now I fear that it may be closer to hand than anyone realizes.

Quickly, I rise from the chair, gather my gown, and take it into the changing room to prepare for the evening and prepare myself to face whatever may come when the sun rises.

What comes is a summons from my father.

He's not come to my rooms to speak with me, and that does not surprise me. With the thrashing of lightning and the darkness that hasn't let up, my mother has not relented. Without justice, she continues to rage. Zeus has unequaled power on Olympus. If he wishes to speak with another god or goddess, they come to meet with him. Only when he chooses.

Beatrice is the one who relays his invitation. We are to dine together in one of his audience rooms this evening. Nerves rack through me. He is the king of the gods, and he has not made it right with my mother. But what justice can be brought? What reason can she see? She is blinded by the betrayal and kidnapping of her daughter and although I am well, I have empathy for her. My thoughts haven't settled and the anxiousness of what might be asked of me is overwhelming. Combined with Hades's warning.

I spend the day with my mother, who has much to say about the plants in the garden. My thoughts choke me. Balling up into a cowardice at the back of my throat. She hasn't brought harvest still. But perhaps the more time she spends with me, the more she will heal. After we have tea and fruit for breakfast, she suggests we go out to her garden beds.

There are hours to go until dinner, so I accompany her to the gardens.

The beds are newly turned over, dark soil warming in the sun. Various pots are arranged on the edge of the bed.

Olympus is empty. Ever since the scry, there is nothing here that holds my attention. All the white walls are a constant reminder that there is a great distance between us, and one that Hades cannot cross.

Realizing my thoughts, it feels as if I've betrayed her myself. My stomach sinks. I should not want the god who stole me. I should side with my mother for how fate has brought me my lover. Worst of all, I haven't the words to confess to Demeter, my mother and savior in so many ways, that I love him and I wish her to stop. I wish for her to accept that there is no justice to give her.

"Ah!" My mother says, a simper on her lips although her eyes are still clouded with pain. "Everything is prepared for planting. Would you like to join me?"

"Of course," I answer, though we are past the usual time. My heart beats quickly, remembering the last time she offered and how my magic and powers has dwindled to nearly nonexistent. "I thought you had planted these beds already," I mention as I pick up a pot and look inside at the seeds it holds. "Did something go wrong?" I play naive, but I am no fool. She's brought death in as many ways as she can for all to see her fury.

My mother purses her lips, moving to the center of

the bed. "I was in a state when it was discovered you were missing," she says guiltily. "I raged throughout Olympus and could not stop. This garden bed was an unfortunate victim."

I reach over and place my hand on hers in comfort. She takes it and squeezes before letting me go again.

"But," she says confidently. "We can plant again."

"Yes," I agree. "That is true. A garden can always be planted again." My throat is tight with any response that I could offer regarding her state and my disappearance. I walk on eggshells around her.

We're quiet for a little while, rearranging the pots, choosing seeds, and dropping them in neat rows throughout the bed. The act is soothing. Healing in so many ways. My intention with every seed is to bring life, abundance, and prosperity to all who need it. Warmth spreads through my chest as the garden grows. I imagine the mortals who suffered for my king's desperate actions to have me. They are innocent and I wish for the growth here to show in their own gardens. As above, so below. *I wish to make them whole again, without parting from what I've gained.*

"Are you thinking the same of the mortal realm?" I question, straightening my shoulders and shading my eyes.

My mother doesn't look at me. She merely whispers, "The mortal realm can be replanted again. It is resilient."

"Is it?"

"Oh, of course." She's still careful not to meet my

eyes. Her pain is evident. The loss echoing in her gaze. As if I can feel what she suffered. The loss is immense. "Much of it is a garden, Persephone. It is only a matter of waiting for new growth."

"When will that come?" I question.

"When my heart is healed," she answers quickly. It's so very evident that she placed a spell. The damage will only stop when she no longer feels the agony. But every spell can be broken, though not every pain can be healed. And my mother's pain I fear will only worsen when I tell her the truth. When I return to him, her bitterness may turn to death for the innocent.

"He will pay for what he did to you," she murmurs.

"Mother," I start, my eyes growing wide. "I don't wish for—"

"It is not my wish, my sweet girl. It is what I need to heal."

"What about the mortals themselves?" Quickly, to keep myself busy, I take up another pot and tip some seeds into my palm. They're small, but will burst with life. They'll become so much more than they appear to be right now. "Will they be able to start again?"

"In time."

I stare at her for a moment, not recognizing her but acknowledging she now knows pain she's never known before. She will see reason. My father will put an end to this soon. He must.

"In how much time?" Perhaps she will be more willing to speak when we are not looking at each other, so I keep my focus on the seeds. "I saw things in the Underworld that made me wonder about the mortal realm."

With concern, she stills and asks me quietly, "What kinds of things, my daughter?" It's then I know her fear of what I had to go through. Her hand trembles and I cannot offer her comfort entirely, but I offer her the truth.

"Souls," I say simply. "There was worry over an imbalance between the realms. If there are too many souls entering the Underworld at once—"

"The Underworld is a vast realm," my mother says, interrupting me gently. "If there is any kind of imbalance, it will certainly sort itself out within the Underworld."

"What if it does not?"

She is silent.

"I wonder," I press on, though my heart is beginning to beat hard, as if there is some danger approaching. "Because many mortals look to me as well, and if there was some comfort I could offer them, some reassurance..."

"You can offer them your presence," my mother says, meeting my eyes at last. "Have you thought of that? It may be more useful than any words you may offer them."

"My presence?" I question.

"Your gift. Your power," she answers.

"Of course," I answer in a whisper.

"We can speak more of it later, for now, please keep me company. I have missed you so," she tells me with tears in her eyes as my own gaze blurs.

"I've missed you as well," I answer.

She smiles at me, a quick, relieved expression, then turns back to the garden bed. "What do you think of this section here, Persephone? I would like something that will be bright when it blooms."

Later that evening, I pace in my room, trying on my pale blush flowing robe and looking at myself in the mirror. I need my father to make a decision on the mess we're in. To offer peace to my mother while honoring the bond Hades and I have made. I do not wish to be in his position or to provoke him, but the warning from Hades makes me question everything. Almost as if I've gone mad.

"Provoke him?" I ask my reflection. "Do you fear his anger?"

Yes, a voice in the back of my mind answers.

I fear my father's anger because I fear that the imbalance between the realms will last longer as a result. I fear my father's anger because my return to the Underworld may be delayed or worse, it may never happen if the war continues to brew.

I'm not afraid of a difficult discussion. I'm not afraid of my own weaknesses. I'm not weak. I'm a queen and goddess. I am simply aware that much of my fate rests in his hands.

I slip on a gown in deep green in favor of my dressing

robes. It's a simple silk piece but elegant. It is not the color of the Underworld, nor is it the color of Olympus. It's the shade of evergreens in the forest, standing firm throughout the seasons. It's the greenery at twilight in the summer. It's the color of growth and renewal.

A few moments before I am to meet my father, I leave my rooms. My mother has gone to her own rooms. I've sent Beatrice to rest as well. In the hall, I hold my head high. The cool breeze is soothing even though the skies are a dark burdened gray. I don't need anyone, mother or servant, god or mortal, to walk with me. As a queen, I can accompany myself. As a goddess, I am powerful in my own right.

My father waits for me in an opulent hall with gilded features on carved marble. The walls are draped with fine fabrics in neutral colors, and low lamps are lit around the room. Zeus, god of thunder, god of gods, king of Olympus, and my father, sits in a regal throne at one end, but rises to his feet when I enter. His shoulders are broad and his posture brooding.

"My daughter." He comes to me with a soft smile on his face that doesn't reach his eyes, his arms open wide to embrace me. I go to him and return his demeanor. He doesn't hold me as tightly as my mother did. It is not a desperate embrace. My father holds me as if we have an audience.

Do we? Knowing Olympus and the games my father's played before, we may. There are many eyes who watch because he commands it so.

When he releases me, I covertly glance around, but there's no one else in the room. This is to be a private conversation.

"Come. Sit with me." His tone is gentle.

He takes my hand and escorts me to a table near an open balcony. The breeze floats through the arched openings in the wall. The air is at the perfect temperature. In the distance, a harp plays and for a moment, it feels like home. We look out on the now soft blue sky, breathtaking clouds that rest on the last of the auburn sunset. Above, the dark sky glitters with stars. It drapes down over the evening like silk. So the storm has passed and there is peace for now.

I'll admit that this view is not one I could see in the Underworld. The evenings there are beautiful in a different way. I am grateful to be a soul who's able to experience both.

Gracefully, I take my seat, and my father takes his own across from me. With a deep call, "You may enter," he waves a hand, and servants file into the room, each of them carrying a covered dish. They place them on the table in an arrangement like a spiral, then whisk the gleaming cloches away. Steam rises from the meal. It smells sumptuous. Decadent. The spices in the air make my mouth water.

"Eat, my daughter," my father says, his tone grand and inviting, and then he reaches for the nearest dish, ambrosia. I'm certain nectar fills his goblet.

For a while, my father chats idly about the colors of

the sky, and the shapes of the clouds, and the flavors of the meal. And how good it is for him to have me home. I answer him with genuine gratitude. I *am* grateful to be eating this food. I am even more grateful that I feel well enough to eat it. That the fear I felt constantly before I went to the Underworld has fallen away. It was a burden and that's what I thought of my presence as well. No longer does it haunt me, but lays heavy in its place. Still I feel peace, for a moment.

But then Zeus reaches for my glass and a carafe of wine. He pours, then offers me the glass. The wine, a deep jewel red, moves side to side inside the crystal.

"Thank you, Father." I graciously take the glass from him and rest it at my plate.

Do not drink the wine, Hades whispers in my memory. *Do not drink from what your father offers.*

Emptiness fills my chest as I hear Hades's warning. Nothing could be clearer. My father chose the glass and poured the wine, then held it out to me. He has offered. I will not drink.

I continue eating, small morsels that I savor before swallowing.

My father says nothing.

Our silverware clinks against the gold plates.

"Drink your wine, my daughter," my father says.

I meet his eyes, making mine wide, as if I am merely curious. "Why am I to drink it, Father?"

The corner of his mouth twitches. "You are to drink it as we always have. It is the drink of the gods."

My father stares back at me, sitting very still, as if that will make me accept what he says.

"If I ask Hecate, do you think she would answer the same?"

Out beyond the balcony, a bolt of lightning sizzles through the air, breaking apart with a loud crack. My father's eyes narrow. "Your disobedience is intolerable."

I arch a brow. "Oh?" My heart races, pushing up into my throat. It did not take much for him to turn against me. It did not take much to inspire that dark anger in his eyes. Why does my father care so much about the wine? "Because I do not wish to drink? That is intolerable to you? What do you wish to do, then, if I am intolerable? Do you wish to send me to the Underworld? Do you wish to tell my mother that you have done so?"

The storm that rips through the sky is as loud as a scream. It rages behind him as he sits like a stone with a glare that could kill. More bolts of lightning tear across the darkness. They're blindingly bright, but I blink until the spots fade from my vision.

The cords in his throat tighten as he swallows. My father sits up straight in his seat, unmoving, as if he did not cause the storm. We both know he did. We both know that it was his anger that burned through the sky. We both know that it was not an appropriate level of anger for questioning a glass of wine. In all my memory though, I don't believe I've ever disobeyed him. Never.

"It would be so easy to see you in the mortal realm, Persephone." My father sounds as if he is mentioning the melody of the harp or the sunset. Something of no importance at all. "Do not press the limits of my grace and patience. Those things come from a place of love."

"Love?" I echo, my breath coming faster. How can he speak to me of love when he threatens to send me to the mortal realm? How can he act as if it was my fault that he lost control? "Such a dynamic and powerful spell."

An angry smile cracks across my father's face as fast as lightning. "Are you only just learning such things, daughter?"

"Is it too late for me to learn?" I shoot back. "I might have learned earlier, if my father had taught me, but he did not. Perhaps he was too busy with his other pursuits."

My father lays a hand on the table, his teeth gritted. "Daughter, do not speak of things you cannot know."

"I believe there is nothing I cannot know. There are only things that have been kept from me."

An emotion I cannot name flashes across his face. It is gone too soon for me to identify. He *is* keeping something from me. There is a secret he does not want me to know. Perhaps many secrets. Anger burns inside of me that Hades did not confide more in me. I'm woefully unprepared.

I open my mouth to demand that he tell me, but another bolt of lightning cracks nearby, forcing a shudder through my body.

No—it is not a bolt of lightning. It is black and dissipates more quickly. In the short distance, dogs bark and the harp is no more. The sky darkens, but two torches are seen. A chill runs down my spine and my lungs still. Several servants scramble beside her, their heads bowed as they plead with her to wait. The dark cloak gathers behind her as the wind blows the thick fabric back. Beneath it lies a saffron garment that's slick to her body. Hecate strides through the place on the balcony where the bolt touched down, her face set. Ever gentle and unaging, yet powerful with a strikingly dark gaze.

"Hecate," Zeus greets her. "To what do we owe the pleasure?"

"Please forgive me if I have interrupted," she states smoothly, her cadence nearly a lullaby. "I came to see the goddess."

chapter 8

Hades

THE WIND IN THE UNDERWORLD WHIPS UP, tousling my hair and tugging at my dark robes as I stand in the dead gardens outside my home. Cerberus leaps at my side. He plants himself in front of me, then runs forward to viciously bark at the sky, all three of his heads making a cacophony. Before howling at the streaks of lightning that blister above us.

It doesn't escape me how he whines when my pain is evident. My dog is loyal. He is trying to warn me. He is trying, in his way, to keep me safe.

I learned long ago that safety is elusive. The only way to have safety is to live in isolation, and even complete solitude is not safety. It can drive one to madness just as easily as it protects him.

I cannot go to Olympus as I am bound to rule the Underworld, but all the realms are tied together by the powers of the gods. Zeus may wish it wasn't so, but there are bonds between our realms. Some things that happen in his realm inevitably reflect into mine.

The bolts of lightning rush across the sky in the Underworld, their color changed by the distance between the realms. The striking violets remind me of Persephone. Everything reminds me of my queen.

The ground shakes as the thunder and violent lightning greet us in unison.

Zeus's anger reverberates through the mortal realm to the Underworld. If it was only his frustration with me, I don't imagine it would make such an impression, but it is my queen he is furious with.

I know it as surely as I know that I need her *back*.

Cerberus faces me, barking louder. He pleads with me to stop the storm that rages overhead. He urges me to *act*.

"Shh, my faithful companion," I attempt to soothe him although I imagine the rage is only just beginning. Zeus has lost the faith Persephone once had in him. I returned her to him stronger and more powerful. Afterall, that is the warning the Fates gave him that coaxed him into poisoning his daughter in the first place.

With stiff shoulders, I force myself to breathe as I watch the symphony of strikes above. The Underworld's murmurs can be heard and their fear felt. I cannot stop Zeus's rage. I can only wait to see if his outburst ends. And wait for it to return.

I cannot stop him or change what the Fates have

decided for us. But it is my duty to aid those in this land. The only fear felt, should be fear of me. And my queen.

I watch the skies for any further sign of Zeus's temper flying out of control.

There are other ways for me to ascertain what is happening on Olympus, but I am in no mood for reaching out through my intermediaries. I suspect that the specific details of Zeus's dark mood are unimportant. There are no other rumors swirling in the Underworld. Zeus can only feel threatened by one person.

My queen. For she knows hints of what he's done.

He should be frightened of her. He treats her as if they're not equals. As if she is still less powerful than he is by virtue of her name, or her lineage, or her time in the Underworld. A deep anger simmers within me.

Cerberus nips at my hand, losing patience with my stillness. It is only then that I feel the clench of my jaw and how anger has tortured my expression into one of vengeance. My faithful companion whines, begging me to move. To do something. He may not understand the inner workings of the Underworld as Minox does, but he knows that things are usually not done by standing in the garden and watching the sky.

"I know," I tell him. "It is quite the storm. You are right." With a long exhale I release the rage for only a moment. "I must do something."

And yet, my thoughts are drawn right back to Persephone. Cerberus whines yet again.

It feels as if Cerberus is the only being in the

Underworld who understands what it is to need Persephone to return. It is like a constant pressure that aches in my bones. It's caused pain every second since I watched her leave.

Yet still my love is stronger than my endurance. My love for Persephone is what keeps the various pieces of me from crumbling. It will hold me in a firm grip until she returns, and then it will wrap her in my obsession as well.

Cerberus curls around my shins, pushing me. There is nothing left to see in the skies. If Zeus rages at her again, if he attempts to harm Persephone…

I will not be the only one who knows. Every being in every realm will know of Zeus's fatal mistake. The tales they tell about it will last for eternity.

With tightly held breath, I turn on my heel to leave the garden and find Minox waiting there, his dark robes snapping at his ankles from the wind. The darkness clouds him. I do not know how long he has been out in the garden, watching me. I do not know how long he has been waiting for me to notice him.

"My Lord," he calls, his voice carrying over the brutal gusts. It's grown stronger now, though I cannot tell if it is because of Zeus or because of the unrest in the Underworld. Chaos surrounds us in all ways.

"Minox," I answer and move toward him, then past him, not slowing in the least. I'm returning to my bedchamber. I need a few moments to think. I need to walk through the halls of my home. I need the familiar floors.

The familiar walls. The familiar doorways. I need to be where I am known and have found stillness and power before.

Minox marches beside me, his hands folded in front of him and his expression neutral. He does not speak, and neither do I. Cerberus goes ahead of us and waits for me to open the door. Then my dog darts ahead as if he's been given orders.

I continue the walk to my rooms. Minox does as well. He still says nothing.

Movement is the only thing that seems to give me clarity, so I don't take the shortest path. I stalk through the corridors of my home, turning one way, then another, treating it like a labyrinth.

If it were a labyrinth, then my queen would be at the center, waiting for me. She would be the conclusion to all my introspection. She would be the place where my mind arrived when it was at peace.

It doesn't make me feel at peace to know that she is nowhere in my home or in the Underworld.

It makes me feel like tearing souls in limbo apart until there are none left to destroy, then starting on the rest of my realms. Clenching my jaw, I force the thought away.

I will not unleash that on the Underworld again. I cannot. Regret runs through me, and I can only imagine what Persephone would say.

Not now, at least. For now, I will walk the halls of my

home, concentrating on my queen and what she would wish, and when I have reached my rooms, I will act.

Minox stays at my side. The tension is thick between us. Perhaps he is in need of a labyrinth as well, because he remains silent as we walk as if he is deep in thought. Perhaps he is. It would not surprise me. Minox spends most of his time in the shadows, watching the goings-on of the Underworld and keeping it running smoothly.

When my queen is restored to me, I will owe him a gift of gratitude for all he has done since she left.

But I remind myself, she has *only* gone so that she may return. She is only gone so that Zeus can feel the consequences of the errors he has made. She is only gone so that balance can be brought back to all the realms, and a truce can be called, and we can resume ruling, as we should have been doing all this time.

It is the way it must be. As angered as it makes me.

It is not until we reach the doors to my rooms and enter that I decide I have waited long enough to hear what he has to tell me.

"I hope it was not urgent," I murmur as I pour myself a goblet of wine. The sound of it pouring against the gold fills the room.

"What are you referring to, my Lord?"

"Whatever news you came to bring me. I assume it was not urgent, otherwise you would have said it by now."

"I did not come to bring news."

Minox glances at me, his brow furrowed slightly. He

seems perplexed yet calm. The hours since Persephone went to Olympus have been a strain on my advisers.

"Then why did you come?"

Minox inclines his head, as if he was expecting me to ask this question. "I came to await your orders, my Lord. I saw the lightning and wanted to make myself available in the event you wanted to send word."

I almost laugh, a harsh, bitter sound, but I do not let it out. The sweet drink sloshes in the glass before I take a heavy gulp and huff a response. Send word to Olympus? Send word to Zeus? Should we scry once again so he can tell himself he did nothing wrong? Should I watch him through the mirror and stifle the urge to smash the whole thing to pieces?

No. No, of course not. The lightning was a sign that Zeus is in no mood to have a civil conversation.

A smirk reaches my lips at the thought. "Your instincts were correct, Minox. I do want to send word."

It's not long before Minox leaves my rooms; I finish my drink and then leave as well. I adjust my robe and crown, before settling on what will likely occur next.

He will be efficient in sending my message. I won't have to wait long for the conversation that is to come.

Stealthily, I head to my andron. Perhaps this is the center of the labyrinth. It is, after all, the only place I can scry with Persephone, but it is not my queen who I have sent word to. My love must do this on her own. I shall wait in the shadows of the depths of her soul to need me. For I will always be there.

As I step inside the andron, Cerberus follows, shaking the night air off his fur and coming to my side. His feet pat rhythmically, the sound is soothing to the anxiousness that heats every inch of my skin. He peers up at me questioningly.

"There's no need to worry, Cerberus. I have responded to the storm. It will not bother you again tonight."

I stroke his fur.

"I *hope* it will not bother you again tonight," I add, because I cannot guarantee that Zeus will remain calm. "In the meantime, I will speak with someone who may be able to make Zeus see reason."

Cerberus barks, all three of his heads chiming in at different times. I let out a short laugh. My mind is wound too tight around Persephone's absence for genuine delight, but it is close enough.

I straighten and wave my hand at the largest grate. The fire had burned low, but it flares again, casting its reflection into the obsidian. The flames lick up the ashes and flicker into a bright light. The sight is a reminder of Persephone's face in the firelight at Olympus. The sunset becoming an ember behind her. The pink, soft folds between her thighs. Her power surging through the glass.

A shiver quakes in me. Her power had been

evident. Zeus's attempt to starve her of it has failed. I have no doubt that he has recognized it, and that is why he felt such fury tonight.

With the flames echoing in my gaze, I know he has only himself to blame for what comes next. Zeus did not need to cower in the face of the prophecy. He didn't have to resort to these machinations to ensure his rule.

A loud crack blisters through my thoughts, and I turn toward the sound. Eerily, calmly, and expectantly. If my heart beats faster, it's because I'm impatient to say what must be said.

Hecate, in all her glory, strides across the andron, running her fingers through her hair and tossing it over her shoulders. The dark robe she wears this evening is reminiscent of the ashes in the fire.

"Send her to the mortal realm," she says calmly, her low voice still echoing against the walls as she arrives at my side of the andron. "Demeter and Persephone can live there until it is decided."

A crease forms in the middle of my brow as I tell her, "You do not know why I have called you here."

"Send her to the mortal realm," Hecate insists. "You know it is for the best."

"I do not."

Hecate narrows her eyes, the darkness knows no depth in them. "Why have you called me here, Hades?"

"It is time for my queen to return."

"Surely, you can see the wisdom in sending her to

the mortal realm. With her mother. A chance for healing and for Demeter to see reason. To see the strength in her child and what good has come."

"There is no wisdom in being separated from my queen. I cannot allow her to stay in Zeus's presence any longer. Not when he fears her strength."

Hecate waves this off. "He fears all his children."

"The problem is that he does not fear me. *Minox*," I call. Raising my voice, even slightly, isn't necessary but in my desperation I am unable to stop myself. I could call to Minox in a whisper, and he would hear me from the farthest reaches of the Underworld and come to my side.

He glides out of the shadows, his form materializing as he steps into the firelight. He lifts his bowed head. "My Lord?"

I'm filled with anticipation that seems wild. Nearly uncontrollable. It is like fire in my veins. A sudden power I had not noticed before. It's like the moment I saw light again after my long imprisonment. It's like stepping foot in the Underworld and understanding, for the first time, that I had a realm to exist in— one that lived and breathed and turned in its cycles. It did not matter that *life* was for the mortal realm. This would be *my* life.

I inhale, and the air tastes the same as it did that day. Brimming with all the power of the souls who dwell here and the attendants who do the work of judging them and guiding them.

"Bring darkness over the world," I order Minox. "Bring the fear of death. Unleash monsters in the dark."

"Hades," Hecate says urgently. Her eyes widen like I've never seen before.

"My Lord?" Minox questions. I expect this from him. He saw the depths of my grief and rage. He saw me tearing souls apart and causing carnage throughout the Underworld. He will want to be sure I am not repeating those actions.

"Do as I command," I say, staring into his eyes. Then I look back at Hecate. "And let Zeus know— Olympus will be next."

Hecate opens her mouth to speak, but there is nothing she can say to change my mind. There is nothing *anyone* can say. If she thought the pendulum had swung, she was wrong. The darkness has just begun.

The only person who could change my mind is Persephone, but Persephone is not here. This is what I must do to get her back. I have known it since I saw the lightning in the sky, glaring at me from Olympus. The mortals always pay the price of the gods. Demeter started this and I will finish it.

Hecate seems to realize what I am about to tell her before I can speak the words. I see the shock flash through her eyes, and then calculation.

Hecate is no fool. She will understand what must

be done. She will not need to be convinced as Zeus needs to be convinced.

"The army of the dead will seek vengeance for violation of the laws," I tell Hecate before she can speak. Before she can try to dissuade me. "I will bring them to his doorstep if he does not honor the law. She has had enough time. Four days and three nights. I must have her back."

chapter 9

Persephone

WITH A SIMPER ON MY LIPS, I STARE AT MY upturned hand. There is no mistaking it. My powers have returned.

I am not sure exactly when I think to reach for them, but when I do, they are there at my fingertips. The spells and prayers come easily, with power flowing through me like water. I run to the nearest garden beds and press my fingertips into the earth, and there is life. Beautiful and vibrant. Whatever I imagine to grow.

Life!

I sit back on my heels on the flagstones next to the garden beds with fistfuls of dirt in my palms. I know I must look just as crazed as I did in those first days in the Underworld, but I cannot control my surprise. My delight? It is a bittersweet joy to be here on Olympus with all my powers restored.

Long are the days that I feared they'd leave me or that I did not deserve them. I earned this. This beautiful gift.

But then—they were never gone, were they? Because the powers were not what mattered. What mattered was how I practiced. How I believed in myself. How I *learned*.

The process is just the same on Olympus as it was in the Underworld, only here, I am not starting at the beginning. I was born with my powers. My mother taught me the ways of them when she taught me to speak.

I open my hands and look down at the dirt there, then put it back in the garden bed.

Then I spool a plant up from it, bringing life in the form of a blooming rose, straight from the earth. And with a snap, I can deliver it to the mortal realm and let them multiply. I give beauty. I give hope in the despair that still lingers. My mother's grasp has slipped. Her pain subsiding.

I might not've trusted my own abilities if I had not gone to the Underworld. I might not've built that sure, strong feeling within me. How could I have? If I had stayed here—

I do not know what might have happened. I might have lost my powers entirely. I might never have learned how to wield my own confidence no matter the realm I am standing in.

I grow flowers in the garden bed in a wild frenzy. If there are seeds, then they spring up at my call like they were waiting for me to summon them. If there are no seeds, I can create one by imagining what it might be like as a bloom. I practice this until I have to lie down at the edge of the garden bed, my body weak with how good it feels to be myself again.

The sky above me, and above Olympus, is a pale blue dotted with clouds. It has cleared, for the moment, but gray clouds in the distance make me wonder if something else is coming. A storm is brewing.

Something else is always coming. That is what it means to be a god, or a living mortal, and even a soul destined for new life in the Underworld. There will always be change. There will always be growth. There will always be death.

There will always be something to face.

I frown at that blue, the tingling enjoyment of bringing so much life to the garden bed fading from my hands.

Would I give it up, I wonder?

Would I give it up to be with Hades? I cannot stop thinking of my love. He's in all my dreams, appearing there the moment I fall asleep.

I need to get back to him. My palm itches for his touch and I must admit, I miss the weight of my crown upon my head.

Slowly, I rise from the flagstones and return to my rooms. The night is quiet and the people are scarce. I wash the dirt from my hands and change my gown, then settle before my altar.

My heart races. The last time I came to this altar, I was taken to the Underworld. I'm no longer afraid to be taken there, or to go there of my own will.

If I am afraid at all, it's because of the uncertainty of what may come. I'm unsettled by my mother's answers or non-answers to my questions. And my father…

I left, my emotions running high once Hecate was content with me and asked for my leave so she could speak to Zeus. The unease spreads through me once again.

Nothing makes sense here. He'd been angry about the wine. He had threatened me with the mortal realm, and why?

I already had to come to terms with the idea that I might spend my days as a nymph. It has always been a possibility that I might choose to spend some of my time in the mortal realm. But my father threw it at me like he was thinking of banishing me from Olympus. *Condemning* me to the mortal realm, not wishing me well on a visit.

I've not spoken to him since. He is the god of gods, but there is always a consequence to every act. I do not put it past him, but I would fight to return to my mother. Just as I would fight to return to Hades. And what of the pomegranate seeds? When will there be a decision on what consuming the seeds would do?

That conversation could be what is waiting for me. I don't think it will be a pleasant one, but it might be polite, at least.

Over wine, I think, gazing at my altar, my gaze soft. Because he wanted me to drink the wine so badly that it infuriated him when I did not.

I push the thoughts of my father out of my head and practice my powers and prayers once again. The repetition fills me with more of that bittersweet joy. I had felt such panic and grief at losing my powers. I cannot help being happy that they are back.

But I wish I could show Hades. I could demonstrate them through the mirror, of course, but scrying is not the same as being in the same room. If he was here, he could put his hands over mine. He could feel the blooms rise up with his own fingers. He could see how truly worthy I am. How I can bring life.

I wish he could.

My mother's scream echoes through Olympus, startling me. I suck in my breath and turn with wide eyes. I put a hand to my chest with a gasp and sit still, frozen, so I can hear if she screams again.

"Persephone?" Beatrice's voice is concerned. "Are you all right?"

I get to my feet, turning to face her as I do. "That was my mother."

We look at each other for a silent heartbeat, and then we both move for the door, walking quickly. I do not wish to run. I know that things on Olympus have been unsteady. I know my mother has taken her rage out upon this place, too. So I do not want to run.

As Beatrice and I hurry down the halls, an earsplitting crack makes me jump again. In bare feet, we pass through a pavilion that's open to the sky, with columns draped in ivy, and we both look up to see the sky torn into two. My mother lets out another scream, this one pure rage.

Both Beatrice and I break into a run toward the god of god's courtyard. We enter the main hall and almost collide with each other as we come to a stop. My mother is on the floor, and Zeus stands over her, his staff to her throat. They are not alone in the hall. Rage brews inside of me. The sight of my mother, laid on the ground with her dress a mess around her. My heart beats slowly as heat rises in me.

Hecate is there as well, her eyes blazing just as hotly as my mother's. As hotly as Zeus's. All the tension of his lightning bolts hovers in the air.

The ground beneath our feet trembles with the threat of a crack as my mother's hand presses against the earth. Threatening the world to quake. Her eyes are narrowed and pained as much as enraged. What has this come to? More tragedy and war? More threats and destruction? My head spins and my lungs fail me. I cannot stand idly by.

I step forward, my hands out.

"Stop this!" I call. "Let her up!" My throat is horse from my cry. My mouth goes dry and somehow I take another step forward.

To defy the god of gods is unwise. But I will not see him harm my mother. I would do anything for her and she for me.

Zeus turns his back on my mother, the cloak whipping through the air as he does. Quickly, Demeter climbs to her feet and stands there, trembling, venom in her expression. I swallow thickly, barely able to glance at her before being forced back to meet Zeus's furious gaze.

"Tell me what happened," I say, keeping my voice low. "Tell me what I need to know."

Hecate is the only one to meet my eyes. "You must return."

I know, I almost say. But my mother cries out in protest. Quietly, I ask again, "What has happened?"

"You ate the seeds," my father snaps. "He owns your soul."

My heart flips over. It's not fear or terror that I feel. Perhaps a little, but it is only from the weight of those words. My mind accepts them as true for a few seconds before it argues back. It's as if I've just asked the question and now I've been given an answer I never wanted.

"Owns?" I question, directing the word to Hecate. My heart rises to my throat as thoughts race through me. Has he deceived me? I know he has held back truths from me. But to own my soul?

My father scoffs at my question.

Hecate does not look at him. "Any life who consumes the seeds is condemned to remain in the Underworld for all time."

I blink at her. My chest rising with my quickening breath. That does not exist between me and Hades. I rule beside him, not under him.

But it is Hecate's eyes that send dread trickling through me. *All time? All eternity?*

What of my home here? My altar? My powers. How else will the world see beauty in color and delicate petals if I cannot provide them? And the prayers, they haven't come again since I've left. But the prayers for children and birth. I can do that. Surely, I am capable now.

When I have felt the warmth of life blooming from my fingertips. When I have felt what it means to be a goddess who is strong enough to answer prayers and worthy of hearing them in the first place. I do not wish to be forced back.

My mother lets out a furious cry and rounds on my father. "*You* did this!" She stalks toward him, brandishing a finger at him, blaming him. "If you take her from me, it will be the last of—"

He practically growls at her. "I shall turn on you, Demeter. Do not forget, I am the god of gods! Or, worse, I'll send you to Hades."

She smiles. It is a sharp, vicious smile that matches the deep color in her cheeks. "And you will see the end of the world."

My father dismisses her with a wave. "Your threats will not save you."

"No, but they will *end* you. Mark my words, Zeus. They will end you and everything you have ever built. You will sit on a throne among piles of rubble. Is that what you wanted?"

Although they quarrel, my mind spins and my breath comes up short.

Any life who consumes the seeds is condemned to remain in the Underworld for all time.

All time. That means all eternity. That means the thing I feared when I was first there, and missing my mother. Having to stay in the Underworld would mean not seeing her again, unless it was through a mirror.

It would mean not having access to my powers, and that is entirely different from losing them because of a mysterious illness or curse. It would mean knowing, for all eternity, that my powers were returned to me in full, and that they are *there* on Olympus and in the mortal realm, but I cannot touch them.

I did not know that when I ate the seeds.

But there had been some deal between Hades and Hecate. There had been… I look to her, but her gaze offers nothing but sympathy.

There have been so many plans made without consulting me, and now I feel I have chosen to give up half of myself without being warned that it could happen.

My mother and father circle each other, arguing, but I cannot hear a word they sneer at each other. Does it matter if my father has done this? Does it matter where the blame is placed, in the end?

I do not think it does. I think it's already too late and it's my fault.

Is it already too late?

Hecate ignores them both, silently making her way to me, stopping close enough that I have to pull myself out of my thoughts and look into her dark eyes.

"They will call you the queen of the dead," she says, her expression solemn. "Because never have so many died for a god."

"I am not the queen of the dead," I argue, my voice going faint at the last word. "I cannot be. I am a goddess of life."

"Those who love you torture souls in your absence."

"Hades?"

"Those who love you," she repeats meaningfully. "Your mother has sent thousands of souls from the mortal realm to the Underworld, and Hades has destroyed nearly as many. He will not stop this carnage until you are returned."

"But my mother—"

"Your mother is Zeus's responsibility. You made your choice, giving your soul to Hades by consuming those seeds and being consumed in return."

Calmly, as my mother weeps in desperation, I ask Hecate, "How can I be returned?" For I will have words with Hades. I will not be sentenced to a life where I am without and cannot do as I wish.

"What if I just have a little more time," I start but I know the cost of such things.

"Daughter," Zeus states clearly for all to hear, striking his staff and splitting the sky with sharp bolts and a thunderous boom. "It is law. And I will not see the realms come undone."

And so it is.

Suddenly, I can hear it—all of their cries. I remember

the sound. Their voices echo in the back of my mind. All of the souls, mourning when they streamed overhead through the dark sky, but now it is twice as loud. The screams of those in the mortal realm who have relied on my mother for life and sustenance and who have been betrayed by her, they send chills down my spine.

They are calling for me, and they are cursing me. They want me to help them, or they want me to leave… to destroy myself as a sacrifice for them. What they do not want me to do is nothing. They do not want me to stand still.

And I do not want to. These are my people. They send their prayers to me. They believe in my ability to help them or to at least comfort them. At the very least, they believe I am worth *something*. They believe I can reach them, or else they believe I can reach my mother and convince her to favor them again.

My throat goes dry and tears prick my eyes. No longer are the prayers for life anew. It's for those who are already in need. Those who need peace in the afterlife and a guiding hand. Balance must be returned.

"My daughter," Demeter calls, her eyes red-rimmed and tears streaking down her cheeks.

"Mother," I whisper. I can barely swallow.

If he *owns* me—if I am bound to return to go to the Underworld forever—then how can I convince my mother to end her battle against the mortal realm? How will I *ever* convince her to stop? Why would she listen?

Zeus… What will his sentencing be? All because she loved me and fought for me. I must fight for her now.

"Mother stop. Please. Give me a chance," I rush my words out to her before turning back to the Titan who has such wisdom and magic.

"What do I do?" I ask Hecate. Surely, she should be able to guide me. "I do not know how to—I do not know what to do."

"The world is at your mercy, Persephone." Those words turn me cold with fear. I thought I had moved beyond that kind of fear, but it is back, returning with a vengeance. "You must decide soon."

chapter 10

Hades

MY CHAMBERS HAVE NEVER SEEMED AS dark as they do now. And silent. Devoid of any soul. Even as I stare at the fireplace.

In Persephone's absence, everything is dark and lifeless, so there should not be blazing fires. There should not be lights. Not until she's in my arms.

I stand near the windows, my feet planted, looking up at the sky and casting directly into the mortal realm.

It takes a great deal of power to send demons to Earth, and it moves through me like the hottest fires that burn in the Underworld; the pain provides a needed distraction but as the darkness consumes me, it's numbed.

The mortal realm will suffer greatly. It may never stop suffering. It is not my wish, but it must be done. The pendulum swings.

With a heavy inhale and my eyes half closed, I cast

again, another wave of baneful power blazes through me, and through the sky, and through all the realms between the Underworld and the mortal realm. Gritting my teeth, I bare the agony.

This is what happens, I think with resentment as I send another fierce demon through the realms to wreak havoc on the mortal realm. To lurk in the shadows and release the fears that consume the souls. *This is what happens when you play your games with me. This is what happens when you keep my queen from me. This is what will happen.*

It is law that she belongs here. If they do not abide by the law of the gods. If the king of gods ignores the truth… All hell will break loose.

I can do this for centuries. For eternities. Why do they think I cannot? What has given them that false idea? Do the other gods think I learned nothing from all those years I spent alone in pits of despair? Do they think it taught me *nothing?* I know how to live in pain and how to bestow it. That is why this is my rightful place. I can stand the depths of depravity. I can endure it.

I learned more than the dark. I learned more than hopelessness. I learned how to survive both and feel content within them. I learned how to bide my time until I could take revenge.

I learned how to go beyond what gods and mortals expect. To deliver horrors. I learned how to keep storing up my anger and my hurt until it transformed into unfathomable power.

They should know that kings will do unfathomable things for their queens.

Is it unfathomable if I can fathom it? Is it unfathomable if I can do it? I cast another demon into the mortal realm and watch it go without feeling anything but resolve.

My anger still burns. It rages. It howls. But I contain it. I turn the wretched feelings into demons and send them to haunt souls in the mortal world on my behalf. I let it rain down on the Underworld as ash. The silence that fills every corner of the Underworld does not go unnoticed. It's as if they are afraid to even whisper their dissent. As they should be.

There's no longer any part of the Underworld that is not covered in the evidence of my loss. Ash coats every wall. Every intricately carved stone. Every valley. It coats every surface that's in any way open to the sky. Perhaps it is my sickness, but I find beauty in the way it cloaks the roofs. It is even beginning to blow in through the windows of my home. If Persephone does not return soon, perhaps the entire Underworld will be buried in it. No one will be able to see what lies beneath. We will build atop the damage or give way to a new kind of death.

My realms have already been transformed in another way.

Fear has crept into every corner and crevice. It seeps into the places that ash cannot reach. For the first time, there is no peace. There is no comfort. There are no voices. Silence covers every realm like a thick, invisible layer of ash. The souls who pray to me pray that I will forget them. They do not wish for me to remember they exist. To be left alone in the state of war.

I sneer at that silent plea. *Forget* them? Forget the souls I have tended to with fairness and compassion all these centuries? Forget the duty I have crushed under my powers? I cannot forget them. I could not forget them any more than I could forget Persephone.

An inkling occurs to me that I may one day become riddled with guilt. If she is returned to me, then I will have to repair the damage I have done to these realms. I will do so if she requires it.

But *forget?* Impossible.

If these souls truly wanted me to forget, they would stop their prayers. Another plea whispers into my ear with a gentle hiss as I gather more of my power and send another demon, this one gaunt but more ravenous, into the mortal realm. They must assume I cannot hear them if they do not speak out loud.

Absurd. I can always hear them. I will always remember them. I am their god, and they will not forget it.

"Send her *back* to me," I snap at the sky, which is shaded in gray with speckles of lit ash, creating a speckling of lit red in the darkness. All this talk of imbalances between the realms, and yet Persephone is not here. That is the first imbalance that must be fixed. With every minute that passes, I become more and more desperate. More and more enraged. Zeus caved to Demeter because of her wrath. Now they will all suffer mine.

With my fists clenched and my blood throbbing through my veins, I summon more magic, waiting with my eyes closed while I draw on the deep pools of power in the Underworld. This will be a demon larger and more powerful than any I have sent before. It will stalk people's nightmares and send them fleeing to me in their sleep. Praying for death. They will not be safe while they dream, and soon everyone left on the Earth realm will know it.

"I will take everything," I say to the sky. "I will take your dreams. I will take your souls while they still dwell in the mortal realm. I will take your hopes and your fears. I will take everything, and then I will rip apart your only chance to be mortal again."

I send another demon.

"You do not hear me, but you will understand," I say lightly. "I will make you understand. All of you, in every realm. You have spent too long refusing to see. Pretending you did not know. But you *will* know."

I send another demon.

"Do you hear your doom approaching? Have you noticed the demon standing above your bed? Did you wake up screaming?"

I send another demon.

Time passes and I refuse to sleep. I refuse to acknowledge Minox hiding in the shadows. I refuse to take leave given I am at war. Ash falls to the Underworld like snow. It forms drifts and piles. It is the residue of all these spells. All my power. I have been so restrained with it, and not a soul has ever known. I've held back my rage and my pain and been considerate in my judgments. The Underworld has never seen my powers like this.

I imagine Persephone standing beside me, looking out at what I have done. At what I am still doing. She will not need an explanation of what is happening to the mortal realm. She will know what it means to send demons there to drive people to their deaths.

She will understand that I had to do this.

But…

She will also touch me.

My whole body shivers at the memory of her touch.

Persephone will not play games with me. She will lay her hand on my arm and say my name and ask me to come to bed with her. She will say, *you do not have to do this anymore, I have returned to you, and I will not leave again.* She will put an end to the choking terror that grows in the back of my mind.

My queen. Not only do I need her, the world needs her to balance me. For they allowed me to love then took her away. Now they will receive my hatred.

I push that promise into the next demon, giving it the features of the fear in my mind. Horns rise from its skull and a tail whips behind it. Grant it the color of passion: a deep red. Give it the name: the devil. It will send mortals fleeing from their houses and into dark waters. It will send them tumbling off cliffs. They will run for their very lives, and they will be right to do it, because they will see all their worst fears in this demon's face.

More demons shudder out of the palms of my hands, faster than the last. I will send them until she returns. I will not sleep. I will not eat. I will do nothing but pull my power together and send it screaming into the mortal realm.

"I'm living in a nightmare." I send that thought with the next demon. "You will live in a nightmare, too. Zeus would do well to pay attention." They will blame him, eventually. It will all come back to him, and he will have to pay the penance for it. When they have had their fill in the mortal realm, these demons will be starved for Olympus.

Demeter floods the Underworld with souls, I return them as demons. This is justice. This is righteous. It is earned. And Zeus allowed it!

Thump, thump, thump. The steady but slow pacing is easily heard between the thunderous births of my undead army.

Footsteps approach from somewhere in my home.

The door to my chambers opens with an eerie creak. It's gentle yet firm.

With a scowl marring my face, I lower my hands and turn to look at whoever dares disturb my work.

A guard. I used to know his name, but in this moment, it does not come to me. Rage blinds me. I turn away from him.

A moment later, he dares to clear his throat. "My Lord."

Slowly, seething, I drop my hands again, the demon

I was creating disappearing into a cloud of ash, and turn around to look at the lone guard. His face is ghastly and sunken in. Nearly skull-like. A guard of the dead. Although his gaze is a piercing blue and as his head turns his mortal features come and go. The cloak he wears is torn but still drags on the ground. It's edges dirtied from the ash against the light gray coloring it once was. He stands as close to the door as he can get. Does he not know that it makes no difference? The door could not save him if I decided I wanted his soul erased for good. Perhaps that's his desire.

Anger simmers within me.

He clears his throat again. "She asks for time." His tone rises a little at the end of the sentence, as if his statement is a question.

The guard must see my impatience, because he squares his shoulders although his voice wavers. "She asks for time, my Lord."

"Who is *she?*" I spit.

"Your queen."

"*Our* queen," I shout. My harsh correction echoes off the stone walls.

"Our queen," the guard repeats quickly, his voice trembling. He stands stick straight, attempting to appear as if he's not terrified, but it is obvious that he is.

It's then I remember his name. His story. What brought him to be a highly stationed guard. Swallowing thickly, I know I cannot go on like this for eternity. I know that. But the knowledge only makes me want to end it faster. To be more extreme.

"How much time?" I question quietly.

"She did not say," he answers. "She simply asked for time."

His answer leaves me wanting. Snarling, I crave to shout at him. To rage at him. To unleash every barbed word from my mouth onto this guard.

This messenger.

I do not.

"I will not deny her anything she asks for that is in my power to give. In that time, I will continue what I have promised Hecate," I tell him, then turn back to the window. "Pass along that message to my queen."

"My Lord," he says. The door opens and shuts the very next second, and his footsteps fade quickly down the hall.

A shuffling sound distracts me. I stop gathering my power to send another demon to Earth and turn again, more rage lighting in me like a new fire. Was I so unclear to that guard? Does he need me to explain a second time? My queen's message was simple. Mine was even simpler. There is nothing more to say.

But it is not a guard pushing open the door to my rooms with his shoulder.

It is Cerberus.

He pads in, his head cocked slightly as if something is wrong in the room, but he does not know what.

"Come," I command.

Cerberus comes, his tongues lolling from his mouths. He pushes his body next to my legs, whining softly to be petted, so I get to one knee and do it properly. I ruffle the ears on each head and stroke his crowns several times each. He has stopped whining by the time I'm finished.

With Cerberus, it is easy. Concentrating on him for a minute has let my rage simmer down until it is embers.

It's not gone, however. I'm not finished. I'll take that heat and make the demons burn with it, and they will carry it to the mortal realm.

"Do you see?" I ask Cerberus. "This is what all this has come to. Demons in the mortal world. I will send more and more until Persephone is returned."

He lets out a chorus of loud barks at her name, wagging his tail.

"Not yet," I tell him. "Soon."

Cerberus stays close to me, his side against my knee, while I send five more demons to the mortal realm. Then ten. He wags his tail without stopping. He must think the demons will bring her back.

In one way, they will. They must. Or else it will be all-out war.

chapter 11

I MUST SCRY WITH HADES. IT WAS MY LAST WISH from my father. Just a little time to appease my mother. A little time before I will obey the law of the gods and return to the Underworld.

As I wait, I'm tortured. My mother's vengeance wrapped in a curse struck through Olympus before vanishing. She will not stop. I know it so. I could feel her agony in the last look she gave me. She thinks there's a way around what is written but there's not. I'm hopeful that Hades may see reason, because she does not. It is as if the loss of a loved one has turned her mad. Although I still exist. I will thrive even. But she feels nothing but pain.

She's not left the courts and her arguments are screamed for anyone who cares to listen…which is all of Olympus save my father.

She claims the divine law not to be fair as the seeds were only eaten as I was leaving. One foot in and one foot out. Half she screams. But she does not want me halved. She wants me to choose. To choose her. To choose war against my lover for the sake of betraying a binding law. "Hypocrisy!" she screams, saying someone broke the law to abduct me. She blames Zeus, she blames Hades, and with the way she looks at me, I fear she begins to blame me as I do not fight beside her.

No one else speaks to me. The gods and messengers bow their heads and avoid my gaze. They do not wish for war, and I believe they blame me more than anyone else.

And then there are the voices. The prayers come at all hours of the night.

I do what I can to soothe those who call for me, but I cannot reach them the way I can reach the garden beds on Olympus. I send my best thoughts, my best spells. I sing lullabies and incantations for them. I tell old stories about persevering through hardship. I remind the mortals, as often as I can, that the world renews itself. That there will always be life after death. But with so much death upon them, they pray for a different side of me. For mercy in the depths of hell. They pray to me, to aid them in ways I knew not how until Hades wrapped his arms around me.

My hand falters at their pleas. Because I'm not there. I have no power in the Underworld while I reside in Olympus. They need me. The prayers are nonstop and they cry for me to help.

At night, when I'm falling asleep, the prayers get louder. I pull a pillow over my head to block them out, but simple cloth and feathers will not stop the sound. Those pleas are directed to me. Right into my heart.

"I know," I whisper to the sobbing woman. She is crying so hard that I cannot understand her words. They may only be the frantic prayers inside her mind, but her crying interrupts it just as it would interrupt her voice. *Fire,* she cries. *Fire destroys us, please, we need water. We need—*Her prayer breaks off into more tears. "I'm sorry. I'm so sorry."

It pains me to hear these prayers. *What am I supposed to do about a fire?* I want to ask. *How can I save you?* I do not know. I cannot grow flowers to cover a house and put a fire out. I cannot call clouds to come pour rain on what is burning, that is for Poseidon.

I sit bolt upright in bed.

I sit at my altar for hours, asking for rain from Poseidon. Surely he has heard the pleas. My own pleas go unanswered…for he does not wish to go to war. Helplessness falls upon me. It is either Hades's or my mother's doing and given my mother's powers… Hades.

No. I whisper the disbelief under my breath.

The prayers never cease. It seems there are more of them, overlapping so that I cannot understand the words. I concentrate hard on my magic. To bring life to hope. To remind them that life is precious and there are cycles, but there is always hope. Tears prick my eyes.

Is this not war against my own lover? To defy the

fear he's created for them? If it is, then I must also be at war with my mother, to defy the starvation she's also delivered to the mortal realm. They will learn of my betrayal. That I bring life to hope. But that is balance. And I will not fail to do my part. With new conviction, I work my magic and the storm that brews in the Earth realm flows through my veins. *We will not give in so easily to death and darkness.*

I do not know when I finally drag myself to bed. The prayers still come, but exhaustion takes me under. There is no rest, for I am far too depleted.

There's a lull in the morning, I think, because it is the silence that wakes me. I sit up, rubbing at my eyes, trying to settle my racing heart. Perhaps my magic worked even in my sleep. My soul is restless.

I swallow a harsh lump in my throat, wet my dry lips, and throw off the covers. I bathe and dress, blinking heavily. I have not slept very long, but another morning is here. On the horizon in the distance is a beautiful sunshine, a golden hue against a pale blue sky. As if my father no longer fights. Leaving the war for only my mother, my lover, and myself.

With shaky hands, I brush my hair and pull it back from my face with a golden tie, then sit down at the table in my room to eat. Bread. Honey. Water. None of my father's wine. It is difficult to eat, but I force myself to do it. I need to keep my strength and my wits. I need to keep trying with my mother, and even with my father.

Most importantly, I need to make a decision.

Any life who consumes the seeds is condemned to re-main in the Underworld for all time.

It is law. My fate is sealed. Although it is not what the Fates promised me. Absently, I chew and swallow another bite of bread.

They will call you the queen of death.

Those who love you torture souls in your absence.

The world is at your mercy.

Dropping the rest of the uneaten bread, I know war is not what I wish. The world is at my mercy, yet I cannot help them from Olympus in a way that will stop the destruction. I can soothe and comfort them and send my well-wishes to the mortals who are suffering, but I have not been able to stop my mother nor Hades from making them suffer. I can breathe new seeds into the earth and call them to grow, but I cannot replace land that has been destroyed. There is only so much I can change from Olympus.

The same is true in the Underworld.

I was learning to use the powers that dwell there and make my own enchantments. If I return, I may be able to bring different comforts to the souls there.

But if I am in the Underworld, the life-giving powers I have on Olympus will be gone. I am torn in the most brutal of ways. For my children need me in both life and death.

And if I refuse to go to the Underworld, I will never have those powers again. I need Hades to promise me or else I fear the prayers will bring me madness.

You ate the seeds. He owns you.

Anger prickles at the thought. How he dared to wish to own me. Yet, in the back of my mind I hiss the truth: I own him just as well.

My mother believes she has her own claim on me. I am her daughter. I will always be her daughter, whether I dwell on Olympus or the Underworld or in the mortal realm. We will always be bound by that tie between us, and I do not want to sever it. I do not want to lose her forever. And if this law is to be abided by, I will never see her again… The very thought breaks my heart. I cannot live without her, and I know she feels the same.

My mother or Hades? Either choice brings war.

The powers of life or death?

Placing my hands on the table, palms up, I take a steadying breath. How do I choose? If I hold the power of life in my right hand and the power of the Underworld in my left—

Which do I give up?

I cannot put either of them down. I cannot even imagine it. Yet Hecate says I must.

I turn my left hand over, imagining a life where I never go back to the Underworld and almost immediately flip my hand back.

Leave Hades forever? No. No! I cannot. Not when I am his queen, and he is my king. Not when he lets me sit at his side and thinks of me as his equal ruler. Not when he gave me everything I needed to understand my own power. Not when I love him as I do, wholly and true. He is my heart's other half.

I flip over the other hand, imagining that I am leaving behind Olympus. Never seeing my mother again. Never bringing life to a garden bed or a field in the mortal realm. Never comforting the mortals who have prayed to me for life and hope and beauty and who believe in me. They call out to me when they are in distress.

I turn that hand back over, too. How could I leave them all? How could I let them pray to someone who was no longer even listening? That would be abandoning a duty that I have as the goddess of rebirth and renewal. Goddess of life and yet now, of death.

I open my eyes to find that they're burning with tears. Ruling at Hades's side had *not* felt like giving up all hope of my powers, but choosing to stay on Olympus forever feels like giving up an essential part of me. The decision is impossible.

I rise from my chair, the wooden legs protesting as I do, and go out to a nearby balcony where I can feel the wind on my face. I breathe the crisp air for a few minutes and allow it to cool my heated cheeks.

Then footsteps approach, startling my aching heart, and I turn to see Aphrodite coming onto the balcony. My sister. In her long pink silk gown and crown of red roses. She's ever a vision of beauty. I did not expect to see her. Not when so many avoid me. I wait for her to speak.

Silently, she lowers herself into the lounge next to where I stand and gestures for me to take the opposite one. I oblige. As she does, the prayers from the mortal realm rise again, as if something had been holding them down. *Persephone,* a voice cries, desperate, and then another.

Why me? I think, in spite of myself. *Why do you ask me for help? Why not one of the other gods? The better gods?*

And then my mother's voice from my childhood comes back to me: *there are no better gods or goddesses, my daughter—there are only differences in our gifts.*

I do not realize that I have closed my eyes against the prayers until I have to open them again. When I do, I draw in a breath and meet Aphrodite's piercing blue gaze.

"Persephone," she says softly. "You have changed, sister."

More prayers rise. I wait for them to quiet. One voice is louder than the rest and very clear. *Persephone, please, please, end the pain! End our pain. Persephone, do this for my family. For my children. We cannot bear it anymore. End our pain.*

My eyes prick with tears. I know one truth; I cannot save them all but perhaps I shall meet them in the Underworld and offer them peace then. When it fades away, I take a deep breath. "Those in the mortal realm beg for me to end their pain."

"Will you?" Aphrodite questions. Her tone is slightly off, and I wonder if the prayers she hears have changed. If some of her disciples plead with her to save them. Although she is the goddess of beauty and love, she is also a warrior, and all the world knows it. She has a vicious side of her, and without it, beauty would not be fought for or fought over.

"I—" More prayers come, these ones quieter than whispers. They are…fighting. Arguing among themselves, I think. I hear my mother's name. I hear Hades's. *It is Demeter,* one insists. *It is Hades,* another shoots back. *It is both of them!* This third voice is more sure of itself. *They have both turned on us! They are killing us for sport! Our lives are only a game to them! Watch—they will keep killing us until there are none left to remember what they have done. War breaks out among us. They play and we end up fighting and blaming each other!*

The voices overwhelm me on the balcony. My limbs refuse to stay still. "I must go inside," I confess to my sister, and I grow lightheaded.

Aphrodite rises with me, offering me a questioning look, and we go inside and down the hall to a smaller chamber with a clear pool of warm bathing water in the center. The windows are cut in slits, so the light falls over the water in a pattern. On shaky legs, I take a seat at the pool's edge, and so does Aphrodite, although more gracefully. I envy her beauty. She knows it so. This is one of the ways to reach the mortal realm. I get glimpses of it through the water. A roof on fire. A harvest rotted in the field. Someone screams. The vision is one that turns my stomach. I never wanted this.

"I do not know how to end their pain," I murmur.

"Are you certain?" Aphrodite questions, her gaze on

my face begging me to meet it. "You do not look so certain, Persephone."

"I *am* certain," I swallow thickly, my stomach feeling hollow, "that I cannot end all their pain."

"Yet you frown when you say so."

"I frown because…it is complicated." It is more than complicated. The choice before me is not one that seems as if it has an answer. Not one that would end the mortals' pain. If I chose my mother, Hades will wage war on all the realms. If I choose Hades, my mother will wage war on any realm she can reach. No one wins. Pain ensues. And I am the cause.

"There you are," my mother says from behind us, entering the chamber. My body sits straighter at her voice. My heart races. She brings the scent of the garden with her. Sun and soil and flowers. "I thought you might have gone, Persephone." Her voice cracks at my name. Her eyes are red-rimmed and her face gaunt. The bags under her eyes tell the story of restlessness. My heart breaks at the sight of my mother.

The prayers pick up again. Many of them have my mother's name along with mine. "I have not gone." I tell her and nearly choke on the words. Yet. The last word that failed to slip through my lips: yet.

I reach my hand out to my mother, and she comes to sit on my other side, peering worriedly into my face. "What disturbs you, my sweet daughter?" she asks, but surely she knows it is not one thing that plagues me.

Hesitantly, I answer with a partial truth. "The

mortals," I murmur, her hand still in mine. "They're asking why you have forsaken them." My lower lip trembles as I dare to look at her. Meeting her eyes and knowing her truth.

My mother furrows her brow, her lips pursing in regret. I watch her try to deny it—try to clear the expression off her face—but she cannot. Have I been here long enough to persuade her to show mercy to the mortals?

"Mother." I squeeze her hand. "Do magic with me." A smile, although soft and one that doesn't reach my eyes, slips onto my face.

"Magic," Aphrodite repeats, kicking her feet playfully under the water. "I do love it so," she reminisces.

My mother's face lights with love. "Persephone," she says. "You've never—"

"I didn't have a chance to ask you before. I did not know enough of my own powers." Aphrodite peers at me as though she knows I have a secret, but she doesn't interrupt. "I thought I might never get the chance to do this with you. Now we are together. Will you?"

She suddenly looks hopeful and shy, as if she also dreamed we might do magic side by side but never had the courage to admit it. "It is time to welcome harvest back to the earth," she muses. "Would you like to call it with me?"

I cannot help it. A grin spreads across my face, and my power grows in me. This is the greatest pleasure for my mother, and for me—

For me, it is *almost* the greatest. I do not know yet if it would surpass what I might find in the Underworld. Dread creeps in at the thought.

I shake off the comparisons. When my mother offers me her other hand, I take it. I can feel Aphrodite watching us, excited for what is to come. Perhaps the start of a truce. Perhaps with my mother's healing, whatever Hades has done will not feel as heavy for the mortals. Maybe they can live with his pain so long as they do not feel my mother's wrath. It is a balance. One I can provide. Hope flows through me.

"For the good of all and to the harm of none," we whisper. Together, my mother and I start the spell, our eyes closed, our hands held by one another.

"With our whispers, seeds crack to listen.

"With our hands pressed, warmth touches the earth.

"With our hearts open, the harvest grows.

"It provides and our spell is met. It feeds life and our divinity is blessed.

"So mote it be."

The mortal realm will be green and lush with new growth as it should be. It has never known such death before. Such coldness. The harvest will grow under the soil, ready to be at its full height soon enough.

With hope renewed, I glance into the pool of water and see the vision we have made. The chill that crept along the ground is already thinning. It will retreat fully soon, leaving the soil open for planting. Green buds appear on the tips of tree branches. The last of the storms my mother cast will leave the land, leaving water behind them, and the rivers and streams will carry that water to where it is needed.

I see the spring that will be, with all its green shoots and early petals and small leaves on the trees. *Spring.* What a word. I see birds returning to their homes and pecking at puddles of water in the sun. I see people walking outside their homes and stretching, tipping their faces toward the sky. It is already happening. It is almost ready to begin. It is not here yet, and it is all around us.

We return life to the mortal realm, which has been so hungry for life. We tell the life that waited there, under the ground, that it is time to reappear.

My mother stops withholding it. She lets the earth begin again, without interference. She plants life through her spells and her powers, and she will let it grow once again.

When it is finished, she's still holding my hands, but she has closed her eyes, and she is smiling.

My heart races with giddy joy. My hands shake. Truly, I did not think this would ever be mine to give to the world. If it is only this once, I will treasure this memory forever. But then there's a thud in my chest. Is she only offering this truce because she intends to keep me here?

"That was wonderful," I say, my throat tight with emotion. "Thank you, Mother, for doing such beautiful magic with me. I thought the chance was lost to me. I—" I am so overwhelmed that the truth comes to the tip of my tongue without any thought behind me. "I thought these powers were lost to me."

My mother opens her eyes, confusion in her gaze. "Because of the Underworld?"

"No. From…" I start but I'm all too aware of Aphrodite's presence. Perhaps that's why my mother plays coy. I straighten my shoulders, no longer wanting to hide the truth. "From whatever caused my powers to weaken before that. Remember how I feared becoming a nymph?"

Aphrodite laughs. The sudden sound startles me. "Because you took them back, didn't you?" With her neck arched, she leans back, as if casually playing with me.

I stare at her. "What do you mean?"

"You took them back," Aphrodite repeats. "You knew they were being stolen by the wine, so now you refuse to drink it. It is a lovely trick."

"The wine?" Chills run down my spine. A subconscious truth writhes within me, begging to be released.

Aphrodite's eyes go wide, and she puts her fingertips to her mouth as if she has said this by mistake and then smiles delightfully. "The poisoned wine," she whispers. "The wine our father gave you." Her blue eyes spark. "You took your power back because it was never something he could take, only a piece of you he could wish to dull. Much like what Hades has done. He can never have you if he forces it."

Anger blisters along my skin.

"Hades cannot have you fully if he forces you. These selfish gods. And all in the name of love…" She sighs, peering longingly into the pool as a mortal pair embraces with the fire closing in around them. "Their prayers are as foolish as their actions."

chapter 12

Hades

I N THE UNDERWORLD, THE SOULS ARE CAUGHT in faded white streaks across the dark sky. Their passings are slower now, leaving only smaller groups behind, and then individual souls. One here, then a pause, and then another. The deaths have slowed and those that appear have arrived with more peace than before. The heartache has softened. Although the stench of fear is ever present in some, there is a sense of normalcy. Of what used to be returning.

There's a churning in my stomach of slight regret but also of the unknown. The doubt seeps in.

I watch from one of the arched stone windows of my chambers, Minox at my side and Cerberus laid on the floor on my other side. Demeter has changed something. We must listen to the whispers. To the prayers that are ever-changing. The gods can rarely hide from one another, for the mortals' prayers come from truth and often desperation.

Cerberus sits up, sensing that something has changed. Perhaps it is the silence that Cerberus notices. The screams and cries have settled. He barks, once, and I pat each of his heads duly and with a soothing hush.

Through the eyes of my disciples and demons alike, I can visualize the mortal realm. At times, it's as if I'm there. It is easiest when scrying, just as it is easiest to see Olympus when scrying. But occasionally I can see into the souls who are passing or those who are close to doing so. I can see the images they hold in their minds, vivid with the colors of the mortal world.

And what I see—

What I see are families huddled together, peering out the windows of their homes. Standing up from where they had been crouched underneath the sills. They are pointing. Smiling. Saying *look*.

What are they looking at?

They are looking at the coming of life. Of greenery on crops that had withered. They see hope and are thankful. They imagine abundance and no longer starvation and crisis. They feel hope. They weep with gratitude.

The ice and snow and fiery storms brought by the demons are fading, and everywhere there is green.

Swallowing thickly, I bring my vision back to the Underworld and meet Minox's gaze.

His eyes have centuries of familiarity to me. Minox

has been at my side since the moment I arrived in the Underworld.

"That is the work of my wife." My tone is even although turmoil is present.

Another glance at the sky. Minox will want to know if the lull in the souls is only temporary or if it is permanent. Nothing is ever permanent, but *this* lull is because of Persephone. I know it in the essence of my soul.

We both stare above us into the sea of souls. For a while, not a single soul crosses to the Underworld. Then one soul, very small, flies overhead like a shooting star. It's graceful as it floats down to the river, disappearing from sight just before it arrives.

"She could never do that while she was here," I tell Minox as I reminisce.

"What could she not do, my Lord?" he questions, his brow furrowed. As if he does not know. Genuinely so. How could he not?

"She could not bring new life to the earth…she could not even do it here. The Underworld only invites the dead." There is a hollow feeling in my chest. It aches, like it is begging to be filled. I miss her dearly. My beloved. Persephone does not need to bring souls to the Underworld, that is not for her to do, and she could not, but I know how much she wanted her magic to follow her here.

"She could not ask life to flourish and start anew. Not in our realm."

Minox nods slowly, understanding. He parts his lips to speak but visibly refrains.

I cannot make the argument that those who dwell in the mortal realm do not need my queen to provide for them. They do. They need new life and renewal. They need a harvest that is not struck down by disaster. They need bounty and abundance. Which Demeter can provide, but they also need new life. New hope. She serves a beautiful purpose to those in the mortal realm.

Yet those who dwell in the mortal realm are not the only souls in existence.

"She is needed here," I state, keeping my voice level. "There is chaos in my realms, and they pray to her as much as they pray to me."

Minox's gaze falls to my face, and I look back at him. Though he stands still, his robes still move from the slight breeze. With it, the ash drifts against the stone wall, reminding me of my recent deeds.

His expression reveals nothing to me. I cannot tell what he is thinking. I only know that he *is* thinking, because Minox is always thinking. He's always calculating.

I do not know what my expression shows him.

His eyes move over my features. Perhaps my face is showing him that I know what it is that *he* knows. The chaos in my realms is not only the fault of Demeter. I have caused chaos here. I have torn souls apart. I have shaken the foundations of the Underworld. I have sent souls scrambling for places to hide.

For a time, they were silent as the ashes fell. None of

them wanted to draw my attention. They feared it. The depth of their terror was felt in silence.

Now, not all of the souls are silent. Some of them have come out of hiding, and they're fighting among themselves. On what has caused this and the threat of war. They argue on who is to blame. This fighting only brings more uncertainty. It only leads to more fighting. More arguing. Soul against soul. It may spread to realm against realm, and then there will be even greater chaos. The sooner she is returned to me and this is ended, the more peace there will be.

In my chest there is a deep ache for her. An impatience that I cannot shake. There were times when I was imprisoned that I felt this way—as if I would lose my mind if I did not have a chance to move, to stretch, to claw at the walls. It was never worth it to spend the energy on those attempts. It only made me more frenzied. It only made me more desperate to get out, and desperation made the hours stretch out into centuries.

"Persephone is needed here now more than ever."

"That may be," Minox says and peers out the window, avoiding my gaze. There's no chaos in my gardens as of yet. The areas of the Underworld closest to my home will be the last to fall, as the souls will try to stay out of my sight until they cannot do it anymore.

We stand in silence. Cerberus gets to his feet and pads in a circle around the room, sniffing every so often at the ash and stopping to listen occasionally. He must decide everything is as it should be, because he returns to my side.

"That *may* be?" I question, not looking at Minox.

"I *know* our queen is needed here, my Lord." He emphasizes the word and replies quickly.

"But?" I urge him to continue.

Minox unfolds his hands, then refolds them. "Demeter says that she will bring death again if you take her back. She is willing to stop now that Persephone has returned, although there was no punishment for her abduction. She suspects Zeus played a part. Her anger has dimmed but only because she has not received a consequence for her reaction either."

The impatience inside of me heats until it has the form of rage once again, then irritation, then disgust.

Demeter would bring death again. Demeter would ruin the harvests in the mortal realm so that thousands starve and die a most painful death. The selfish goddess will not feel her loss alone. Demeter would burn the silos where grain was kept. Demeter would turn the mortals against each other in wars for food and water.

Demeter would make the sky above the Underworld bright with souls. Demeter would send so many that they would overwhelm the rituals in place that keep judgments fair and swift. Demeter would make my realms too full of souls, too crowded, too uncertain. It will crumble. It will fall apart. And Persephone would not be able to take those souls back to the mortal realm… not while she's beside me.

Demeter would do all that—to the *mortals*—because I had gotten what I wanted.

What I *need*.

Demeter will not stop there. She will bring all the realms down on one another. There's only so much death she can bring to the mortal realm before there will be no one left. Souls cannot leave the Underworld, and they are trapped here for all eternity. There will be no rest.

When all the mortals are dead, the Underworld will die, too. It will stagnate.

And so will Olympus. Has Demeter thought of that yet? The souls in the Underworld do not pray to the gods and goddesses on Olympus. They do not need Persephone to bring them life because no life dwells here. They do not need Demeter to bring another harvest to the land because the Underworld has all abundance.

What will the gods and goddesses on Olympus do if no one prays to them? What entertainment will they have if they cannot influence the mortal world with their whims? If there is no one left to light candles at their altars…what will their purpose be?

Perhaps Minox suggests that I could save all these realms by giving up my rights to Persephone.

That cannot happen. Persephone has eaten the pomegranate seeds—I have a *claim* to her. It was accepted by her. She put the seeds in her mouth and ate them before my eyes.

And she is my queen. She has sat next to me at court and judged souls. This was no secret to her reign and entitlement. The souls here know that Persephone is their queen as well as mine.

Give up my claim to her? Never. Give up being able to see her face and touch her and kiss her? *Never.* To have her in any and every way she pleases… We have yet to discover how many ways I can send lustful chills down her gorgeous curves. There is so much more between us.

It's too late, since Zeus has agreed to send her to me.

Would Demeter give up her own life? Would Zeus give up his power? Neither of them would do such a thing, so it is ridiculous that they would expect me to give up Persephone. She is more than my life and more than my power. More than anything else that exists.

She is mine.

Once again, I meet Minox's gaze and his expression shows nothing.

I'm not the one who has gone back on my word. I am not the villain for insisting that Zeus stands by his promise to me.

I'm not the villain for using everything in my power to enforce the agreement. Zeus was barely thinking when he spoke to me. All he wanted was to relieve his own fears of his offspring's magic becoming more powerful than his own.

Zeus did not want his daughter to surpass him. Zeus did not see that she had already surpassed him by existing in his realm. Here, she is no threat to him. More powerful or not, she is no concern to him.

Persephone has accepted her role as queen. She

has eaten the pomegranate seeds. She has slept in my bed and kissed me with passion that cannot be undone and opened herself to me so completely that we will be bonded together forever no matter where she goes.

And I will stop at nothing for her.

My love will always be greater than my anger, but that is not all. My love will always be greater than *anyone's* vengeance.

Zeus's.

Demeter's.

All the gods and goddesses on Olympus. All the mortals in the mortal realm and all the souls in the Underworld. All of their anger combined could not outweigh my love and need for her. They'd have to destroy my very soul before I relented.

The sooner Demeter recognizes she will not force me to let Persephone go, the better. The sooner Zeus understands that he cannot give his word without meaning it, the better.

The sooner all this violence will end, and balance can return to the realms.

If they choose not to see it? That is their choice, I suppose. They can remain cut off from the truth if that is what they desire, but it will not bring them peace.

I glance at the door, but Persephone is not there. Not yet.

"If Demeter says she will bring death again," I say finally, looking directly into Minox's eyes, "then death shall come again."

chapter 13

Persephone

I F APHRODITE AND MY MOTHER UTTER A WORD to me, I don't hear it. There is only ringing in my ears and anger in my bones that moves me.

They might. Distant voices echo in the room, as if I am listening to them from deep underwater. Nothing reaches me, though. The only words that reach me are the ones Aphrodite spoke just now.

The words change directions and try to rearrange themselves into something else. Something understandable. But there is nothing to misunderstand about the sentences. They are too simple.

The poisoned wine. The wine our father gave you.

My mind wars to make them separate things.

The poisoned wine.

Yes, that makes sense. Wine that is poisoned would weaken my magic. That is why it left me. It didn't abandon me. It was forced out and I was too naive to know. It could make me feel weak and distracted. It could make it very difficult to decide what to do and even harder to fix the problem.

If I drank poisoned wine for long enough, it might take several days, or even weeks, to leave my blood entirely. It might follow me even into another realm, leaving me sick and weak until its effects could finally wear off.

Poisoned wine would explain what was happening to me on Olympus, and it would explain how it slowly seemed to reverse in the Underworld. I would never have the use of the same powers there, so it would not be clear, truly, until I came back to Olympus and had everything back again.

It is the second sentence that does not fit.

The wine our father gave you.

That does not make sense. My eyes narrow. Although Zeus may be cruel, he has never attempted to harm me. Never. And why would he? What have I done to deserve his wrath?

My father *poisoned* me? My father gave me wine that would eventually kill me or leave me without my powers? My father gave me that wine, over and over, every time I sat at a table with him? Was it all poisoned? I've drank it for as long as I've known.

I always drank the wine my father offered me. I did not have any reason to think he would give me anything to harm me. I can picture my hand in a hundred different shades of light, morning and afternoon and evening.

Night, with the glow of sconces on the walls casting a shadow onto the tablecloth along with the clear outline of the glass and the dark-as-blood color of the wine.

I'm reminded of the anger on his face when I challenged him. Hades gave me enough to know that *something* was wrong with the wine my father offered me, but he did not use the word *poison*. He told me he could not speak of what he knew, but insisted that I shouldn't drink the wine. How did he know? My rage burns for Hades as well. How could he have known and why was he not foretelling? Men who claim to love me…what have they done?

Why couldn't he speak of what he knew? Why could he warn me, but not tell me the full truth of what had happened? How does he *know* the full truth?

Thoughts race in my mind as my breath comes heavier and heavier and my vision turns red.

Is the Underworld part of this, too? Who else knows? My sister Aphrodite, Hades, my father. I turn to gaze upon my mother. Does she know? She couldn't have. Not her. Please. Not my mother as well.

With my throat tight, I cannot speak. For if she confesses I know not what I'll do.

A righteous anger grips the mourning that flows through me. I feel as if I should be surprised, but I am only surprised that the news has come now, and so easily, from Aphrodite. *She* does not seem to wonder if what she says is true. She is not passing along a rumor. She knows this for sure. Zeus gave me poisoned wine and Hades knew.

I rise from my seat so quickly that my mother gasps.

"Persephone," she whispers my name and reaches for me. "Stop."

"No," I answer with my jaw clenched and a madness racing in my blood. "I need to speak with my father."

"What did you say to her?" My mother asks Aphrodite, as if she is hearing what Aphrodite said after a long delay. "Did you say *poisoned?*"

"Demeter," Aphrodite begins, and I do not stay to hear what she says. I've heard enough.

Their voices follow me as I move through the halls, echoing again. I'm not paying attention. The conversation they're having will catch up with me, or it will not. All that matters is finding him. Confronting him. The god of gods acted to harm me. With my fingers outstretched I'm vaguely aware that the ivy that traces along the arches bursts into thorns. The once vibrant petals of florals turn a deadly black as I move through Olympus.

Murmurs of those around me mean nothing so long as they move out of my way.

With a shove of my hand nowhere near the doors, the ancient and carved wood cracks open violently at my arrival. I stride through, nearly blinded by rage.

Poison me? If he wishes to kill me may he strike me dead for all to see! May my wrath bring upon poisonous spores for him to breathe! As my heart pounds, I'm made aware that the hall is filled with people. My father sits proudly in one of his thrones on the dais. Beside him is a man who has Zeus's attention.

Whatever he requires of my father, it will wait.

"Father," I call, making my voice loud enough to cut through all the remaining conversation in the room. The hall goes silent at my interruption.

"Look." A servant gasps as she points at me. It's then I feel my crown. What once was a floral wrath upon my head is now consumed with flames. My fingers twine with their warmth. I peer down at my pale chiffon robes to find them a seething red.

The shadows of the darkness overcome my light.

"The dark queen," the servant whispers in reverence until my narrowed eyes meet hers and then return to Zeus, the object of my rage.

I do not wait for him to look up as he seems to refuse to meet my gaze. I stride toward the throne as he reaches for his staff and the skies above us darken. Gods and mortals alike move aside as I approach the dais. I have not come into the hall like this before. I have *never* barged through a crowd without waiting to see if they would move for me. I have only one goal, and it is to reach my father and settle things between us.

He will never harm me again. That I am sure of.

The person who is speaking with my father—I do not even bother to see who it is—whirls out of my path as I stride up to the dais. I do not see where they go. I do not look to see who is watching. I plant my feet in front of his throne and stand up tall.

"Poisoned wine?" I breathe the accusation. "You dared to serve me poison?" With an arched brow I speak more clearly, sure that those in the hall will hear. Their hushed whispers are my confirmation.

My father waves a hand lazily in the air as if it is not truth spoken. "You are not poisoned now."

"You poisoned me. *You* did. With wine. Why did you wish to harm me?"

Anger flashes in his eyes. "I would not harm you, daughter. Everything I've done is out of love for you—"

"Liar!" I scream and the gray skies blacken. My father's grip on the staff twists and the vines along the carved marble twist into thorns, growing and weaving closer to the throne.

"Speak the truth!" I demand in a hoarse scream.

My father leans on one arm of the throne, looking down at me like my rage is not warranted, as if I'm only here to bother him until he can swat me away to the mortal realm. "What does it matter in the end?"

"That you *poisoned* me? It matters quite a bit, Father," I practically spit.

"You love him, yes?" he questions and my eyes widen. The audacity for him to pretend that he aided in a beautiful endeavor rather than one of deceit. I'm struck by his arrogance and the way he twists his actions.

"All I ever did for you, was to ensure you would be loved forever."

My lips part to answer and find that I am shocked

into silence. I was not expecting such excuses. And—love? When my heart aches tirelessly for my lover.

But then, in the beat of silence, I peer at my father's expression. This past week has aged him and there's no doubt there is affection in his gaze. Even a plea of under-standing. As well as the hope that I'll admit it, for all the hall to see. Including my mother, who holds her hand to her mouth in the corner of the room as she stares at me.

He watches me, eyes narrowed, seeming…almost impatient. As if he already knows *my* answer, too. As if I am wasting his time by refusing to answer immediately. He already knows.

"Yes?" he says again, with a tone that says *quickly, Persephone, I am the center of Olympus, and I have many other things to do.*

"I do love him," I admit. "But—" The hall erupts with hushed whispers.

"I knew you would. I merely planned for you to meet him in a different way than you did but to always be loved and protected. You know as well as I do, if you'd stayed you would have been lessened to merely a gar-den nymph!" He raises his voice as his argument picks up steam. "What I did to you, I did *for* you," he states, his dark eyes piercing into me, almost paralyzing me.

He wanted me to meet Hades another way? The wheels of my mind spin as my insanity twists around my consciousness.

There is only one other way I could have met Hades, and that is by being sent to the mortal world to become a mortal and then *dying*. I would have had to lose my status as a goddess, then succumb to something like *poison*. Then my soul would have gone to the Underworld, like every other mortal soul.

"A different way?" I whisper with my head tilted. "A way where I did not have *magic*?" My anger simmers within me, and a fire burns outside the window. Erupting and causing screams of terrors. Buckets of water are quickly brought but the fire grows, surrounding the hall.

My father turns to see the flames, then glares at me. "Do you threaten me, daughter?"

"You wanted to take this away from me? My purpose? My very being!" I shout with tears in my eyes.

There are voices at the entrance of the hall. My mother is louder than Aphrodite, but Aphrodite is not much quieter—and there is a third voice with them.

Athena. Her demanding voice ever commanding attention.

"Do not be angry, sister!" Athena says in a tone that is probably meant to be pleading. Or soothing. "He only tries to kill his favorites," she adds.

"I do not *care*," my mother snaps. "Persephone is my *daughter*. How dare you suggest to *me*—"

Aphrodite cuts in. "How could you not know? It was so obvious! How could Demeter's daughter suddenly be without powers? You had to be waiting for this, Demeter! He never wants to allow—"

The gods of Olympus argue by his throne as I glare up at him. My fingers stretch one at a time in a pattern before coming back into my palm and all the while the plants wait for my call. With patience I stand before him. My anger dimming with the thoughts of Hades.

He knew. He saved me and yet… He knew.

My father huffs, loud enough to draw my attention back to him.

"What's done is done," my father says, clearly finished with the conversation.

I am not finished. But my anger is so strong that I do not know how to form an argument that will cut as deeply in him as I feel now.

I crave to *hurt* him when I speak. I desire to make my father feel ashamed of what he has done. Although shame is not something he is accustomed to and surely, this is not the worst thing the god has ever done.

Perhaps Athena's comments have merit. I desire to make him understand that he has damaged things between us beyond repair, and it will never be the same as it was. Perhaps I was a fool to not see him for who he is truly to his core.

My father and I have never been close the way my mother and I are close. He did not spend the kind of time that she spent with me in childhood. He did not teach me magic the way she did, with a shared warmth between us, as if she was inviting me to come with her as I began to discover my powers.

I glance at her and it's obvious she has thoughts of her own. Brooding in the corner, she stares down my father. Her own fingers stirring beside her. Her power is radiant and focused. She does not see me. In an instant she turns her attention to the ground beneath her. But it does not move and she restrains herself. Perhaps she suspected. But now she knows.

My love, Hades's voice murmurs in the back of my mind. *You must come to me.*

Hades. He lures me to the depths of the Underworld. Does he feel my pain at this moment? Does he know I am aware of at least one secret he's held from me?

I came here to know the truth and now that I have it, I turn my back on my father and leave the gods and their pleasures behind me. As swiftly as I arrived, I leave.

My blood cools and the heat upon my crown settles.

I arrive at my rooms before I have even decided to go there. Once inside, I throw the door shut behind me, and as soon as I turn, I come face-to-face with Hecate.

My heart hammers. I might have expected Beatrice, but not Hecate. The great Titan and goddess of magic and knowing. After a few quick breaths I'm able to speak. "Hecate." I greet her with a slight bow of respect.

"My child." She greets me back as she does so many of her followers.

"It is the eve before the new moon," she states in an even voice, and the pounding in my heart beats with anticipation. Hecate would not be here, telling me the phase of the moon, if she did not have something in mind. "I must return to the Underworld for Diepnon."

I hold my breath.

"You are welcome to accompany me, if you wish." Chills run down my shoulders.

My eyes burn with fresh pain at the thought of my mother realizing I've gone, but surely she will understand.

With my throat tight I dare to ask Hecate, "And would you take me back here if I were to ask you in the morning after the new moon has settled? When you lead the army of the dead back to the Underworld… if I were to meet you and plead for your help along the crossroads?" I swallow thickly, aware that I am asking such a powerful goddess if she would ignore the law of the gods if only I asked.

My heart pains in such a way I cannot describe. Tortured between a liminal space.

"I will accompany you for as long as you need," she answers as if she knew I would ask.

I reach out for her hand and the Titan embraces me. The tears fall as I know my mother's agony will be wretched.

And then I hear Hades call me his love once again like a whisper in my ear. As if he's placed a spell on me, I must return.

"Please," I say, relief warming me like a roaring fire. "Please, take me with you."

Hecate glances at the door to my rooms. "It is hours until the moonrise. I will lead my hounds when the moon is fully in the sky. We will have to remain out of sight until then, and no one must see us leaving."

chapter 14

Hades

THE GARDENS REMIND ME OF HER. ALTHOUGH they're only crystals shaped to form petals laid in emerald chips, I'm hopeful she'll love them. They won't be a reminder of what she's lost, but rather a reminder of her power and how she changed the world. My thoughts drift to kissing her neck and the loneliness that I've felt without her when there is a *crack* in the sky above me.

The sound is muffled by the walls of my home, but I wheel around to look in that direction. Cerberus barks a joyful sound, as if someone has come home.

As if Persephone has come home.

Shadows move across the windows inside. Firelight flares in my rooms. I take one step toward the house, then another, and then I have no choice but to stop, every piece of my being on edge of what might be.

Every sconce on the walls inside is lit, and there are fires lit in the hearths. The flames get brighter in a pattern I can see from where I stand in the garden. The light follows a path down the hall outside my rooms, then rushes across a floor below, then another, until it streaks across the ground floor and bursts out the garden doors.

My queen has arrived.

Persephone. My heart falters for a few seconds at the sight of her silhouette, but it is more than enough. Her curves are undeniable. Her long hair blows in the breeze. Her shadow moves gracefully, and at first I'm struck by her beauty and grace. My memory did not do her justice.

My queen is home. She has returned to me. She is here.

The breeze carries the murmurings of a conversation and before I can even move, she picks up the hem of her gown and runs. Toward me. Persephone's steps kick up ash as she goes, throwing a cloud of it into the air.

Again I'm struck by the thought that it's a dream. My love. She *runs* to me. Her steps are light as she rushes down the garden path toward me. With my arms out, I erase the distance between us, craving her more and more with each beat of my heart.

Is she real? She *must* be.

Then the starlight catches her face, and it is my queen. She is here. The curve of her cheek begs me to brush my thumb over her soft skin.

There are a few final seconds where there is still space between us, and then Persephone is in my arms.

Where she is meant to be. Her embrace is everything my shattered heart needed.

There is no hesitation in the way we come together. I throw my arms around her, and she throws her arms around me, scrambling up onto her tiptoes to loop her arms around my neck. My love. My heart races and my blood heats. My love has returned to me. I've never felt such relief, such a feeling of completion.

Persephone drops kisses all over my chin and neck until I put my hand on the back of her head and pull her in for a deep, fierce kiss. I'm hungry for her. Needing her love more than I need air. Her legs lift with the kiss, wrapping around my waist, and I groan into her open mouth.

My queen. She clings to me.

All I can do is taste her. I've been starving for her. I've died a thousand deaths without her. I've been condemned to an eternity in the dark without her, and I did not know how close I was to insanity until I could kiss her again. With every thought of losing her again plaguing me, I hold her close to me, my heart beating against hers. My grip is ever moving with my hands on her back, under her ass, around her waist. It would not matter if I let go, because Persephone has her legs wound so tight around my waist that she would not fall.

She kisses me back with equal ferocity, her body arching into mine, the heat between her legs pressing into my waist. Persephone threads her fingers into my hair and grabs it in her fists. Forcing a hint of pain that intensifies the pleasure. *Fuck me.* I've never been this hard for her. She slides her hands around my neck and tugs me closer. Her nails gently scratch as she goes. It's heaven. *She's my heaven.* She grips my shoulders, then my face, panting into my mouth.

"Is it you?" I ask, my voice hoarse with all these days apart. Nothing has ever felt worse. Nothing has ever been more torturous than having Persephone on Olympus. "Tell me it's you, my queen. Promise me it's you. Not some trick or spell."

"I'm not a trick." She breathes with a twinkle in her beautiful eyes, and then kisses me so deeply she can't speak. She tastes like honey, and her skin carries the scent of flowers and sunlight, and this is everything she is. My queen is life and warmth and a beating heart. She pulls away for a moment, breathing deeply, her chest rising. "I'm here. I came with Hecate. She brought me back."

"Hecate," I repeat, my mind slow to understand anything beyond my embrace with Persephone. Slowly, I register what's happened. Hecate did not betray me, then. "She stayed with you?"

Persephone makes a needy sound and kisses me again, seeming as if she has forgotten my question. I've almost forgotten it, too, by the time she tilts her chin and looks me in the eye. She settles her weight more firmly into my arms and gazes into my eyes, stroking my hair back from my face and tucking it behind my ear. "I… what did you say?"

"Hecate. Did she stay with you?" More thoughts race

in my mind as I swallow thickly, imagining my queen on Olympus. I've only known stories of her laughter and beauty she brought to the heavens. Images of her from the dark pool of water.

"She was not my chaperone in Olympus. Surely you know the Titan was not needed there where—" She drifts and then clears her throat before looking me in the eyes once again. Persephone shakes her head. "She was there when it counted. She was there when I needed her. She brought me back, and they don't know. We hid in the garden."

"What garden?"

"I used to go to this place in the garden when I was a child and wanted privacy. No one knows about it. Not even my mother. So I waited there with Hecate until the moon rose, and then—"

Then I *know* what happened. Hecate bends the crossroads to her desire. She moves between realms with her hounds. And she did as she has for centuries. Hecate, the mistress of the dead, came back to the Underworld with the sliver of the moon before it turned dark completely, and she brought my queen with her.

As I gaze into Persephone's eyes, I fall into the depths of them. My need to love her turns ravenous. Hecate can take what she needs from this place, for at this moment, I am an absent king. I need my queen and that is all I know.

Persephone cannot speak anymore, although she doesn't try to. I have my mouth on hers again, and I cannot stop tasting her. With one hand and a snap of my fingers, I form a silk blanket from the ashes on the ground and lower us both down so that I lie above her.

She blinks, her eyelashes fluttering, and strokes my hair that's fallen again. One kiss is tempting and the sound of it fuels me for more. Her hair is spread out under her on the blanket like a halo. I kiss her lightly again and this time a flush rises from her chest into her cheeks. Light glows on her face. It is from sconces in the gardens around us, but it is a low, pleasant light and was not burning until she came. She brings light to my darkness.

Persephone searches my face, tracing her fingertips over my features. "It felt like forever," she murmurs. "It felt like lifetimes."

"Yes." I lean down and kiss her again, trailing my lips along her jaw to the side of her neck. "Longer than forever. Eternities. I could not stand it."

"Neither could I," she agrees with a quiver in her voice. "I couldn't…I…"

Persephone's eyes widen as if she is awestruck by me. As if she has never seen anything more beautiful. As if I am the only man she has ever wanted like this. It is true—I am. There was no one else before me, and there will be no one else after me. I will not let her go. I will *never* let her go. "I…I need you."

There is more she wants to say. I can tell. So I kiss her neck and suck softly at the flesh there, feeling her breathe faster. I drag my lips up to the tender spot just beneath her ear and suck there as well.

"Hades." She breathes my name and my cock throbs.

I drag my lips over her skin now, down to her shoulder, pulling the neckline of her gown open to expose the tops of her breasts. "You are my queen no matter where you go. On Olympus, in the mortal realm, in some other realm no one has discovered…you would still be my queen. You *will* be my queen. Always."

"Don't—" She shivers as I pull her neckline down farther, until both of her breasts are exposed to the air and her rose colored nipples pebble. "Don't you—oh." Persephone gasps as I breathe above her right nipple, then directly onto it, then close my mouth over it. "You are my king," she says in a rush. "Wherever I go. There is nothing that can stop you from being my king."

A groan leaves me from deep in my chest. I nearly lose all composure. "Say it again."

Persephone repeats "You are my king," and I bend my head to hers to kiss the words out of her mouth. Deepening it and losing myself in her touch. She arches up to me, her hips rocking against mine, and I cannot hold back.

I need her now.

With rough fingers and a primal need, I push her gown up to her waist and kiss the insides of her thighs as I tear open my clothes. Persephone braces herself on the blanket, watching me, her lips shining in the garden lights, her eyes sparkling, and when I kiss her other thigh she reaches down and pulls her gown higher and higher until she works it up and over her head.

Then she is naked in the garden, and it is right—it is the place she belongs, in my realm, in my garden, underneath me, writhing with need.

She spreads her legs for me. I do not hesitate. I need to kiss her clit, too. Loving how she moans when I do. I suck her and in response, her fingers fly to the back of my head, holding me there with unadulterated greed. I need to taste her sweetness, even stronger between her legs, and lick her clit as she gasps. Her thighs press into my head once, then twice, and then she threads her fingers into my hair and pulls me away until I am back at her mouth again.

I kiss her own desire into her mouth and drag my cock through her soft folds. I could come from that feeling alone, and I let myself linger in it for as long as she will let me. Teasing and preparing her for what's to come.

It is not long before she tilts her hips and I sink into her, letting out a low groan as I do.

"Persephone," I manage. "My queen." My forearm falls to the blanket above her head as I rock myself inside of her, forcing myself deeper and deeper as her back arches off the blanket.

She's tighter than I remember. Hotter. Wetter. There's nowhere else I want to be. Fucking hell. She is everything I need. There is nothing else I can think of. Only her body accepting me as I thrust in hard. And then harder. Forcing small gasps from her sweet lips. I grow with every thrust, holding my breath and fucking her like I need her to come on my cock just to live.

Persephone cries out, her muscles clenching around me. She holds on to me when she can, but her grip moves to the blanket as I fuck her. Clenching the silk and pulling as if it will save her. She writhes under me, arching her neck, and I kiss her there as I fuck her mercilessly. She takes me as deep as she can. She comes with my name on her lips, then a cry that is not any word at all, just an echo of her pleasure.

I kiss her until I must stop to breathe, but I cannot stop fucking her. My body demands it. The sound of her. The sight of her. The taste of her. I take it all, and I will never get enough.

I fuck her as if the depravity of it would chain her to the Underworld. *Mine.* All I can think, as she cries out my name and her nails dig into my back, is *mine.*

Persephone comes again, gushing on my cock, and I want to keep fucking her until all my realms end. Until Olympus comes down and shatters into the Underworld. Until the mortal realm becomes one with this one, and there is nothing left in the world. It could all happen around us, and I would not want to stop.

I hold her to the blanket and bury myself deep in her, as deep as I can go, and though I want it to last, my release takes over.

I've never had a more powerful orgasm. It is all my need and love and worship for her.

Persephone lifts her head and presses her face in my

shoulder, her legs shaking. She trembles with the force of our union. In the quiet afterward, the only sound I can hear is her frantic breath.

Then she says something too soft to hear.

"What was that, my queen?"

She lifts her head from my shoulder. "Again," she whispers and then kisses me sweetly.

"My ever demanding queen," I murmur against her lips and then thrust my hard length back into her sweet cunt.

chapter 15

WAKING TO THE MEMORY OF LAST NIGHT with the soft light of the rising sun brushing my face, I know one thing: I needed him. The pull to him was unrelenting the moment I found myself back in the Underworld.

I need him *now*. I cannot wait to touch him, to see him, to make sure he's still here.

He was still the same, but I could see that it hurt him to do what he did. Hecate told me everything. She prepared me for the ash. I did not know how he would embrace me given his chaos.

But Hades's mouth against mine was everything I needed and the most delicious thing I have ever tasted.

Having him move against me, inside of me, and give me all his pleasure, there on that blanket—that was what I craved every second I was on Olympus. I needed that time together. I needed him to move within me with all his strength, showing me that he was still my king. That he was the god I fell for and that he still wanted me too.

My heart beats slowly as the voices murmur softly around the castle.

There are fewer souls in the Underworld around his home. I did not know it fully until he took me inside the house last night, and then I also understood why.

Ash was everywhere in the Underworld, covering everything.

But, as it was on Olympus, my powers were there at my fingertips. I did not have to struggle to use them. I did not have to worry about them or pray to be allowed to have them.

I simply raised my hand and let my powers do what they needed to do, and what they needed to do was swirl over everything, clearing the ash away.

It is like bringing life, but it is not the same. It's hard to describe. It was the erasure of the destruction. To bring warmth back to the chill and light to the darkness. Nothing new grows in the Underworld—nothing is actually alive save the souls themselves, which I cannot create here—but what exists can be changed. The magic turned ash to diamonds and quartz creating paths now embedded with beauty to guide those in this realm.

I didn't ask Hades about the ash as he took me to bed. I knew from the look in his eyes that he would need time. All that has happened has been a nightmare for both of us, but especially for Hades, who could not follow me to Olympus.

"I would have," he says against my shoulder as we lie in bed, leaning against the silk pillows with the sheets gathered around us. I rest my back against his strong chest. He strokes his fingers through my hair, working out the tangles he caused when he was over me in bed, and some of the ones *I* caused when I rode him, feeling the new angle of him inside me, learning the ones that gave me the most pleasure. "I would have come to you. I'd have broken the laws and allowed them to destroy my very soul if I could not have you again." He whispers the wretched words.

"I know," I answer simply and cover his hand with my own. My fingers slip through his. The calluses are rough against my soft skin. Hades flexes his fingers every so often. I don't think he fully believes that I have returned.

I have.

Though I do not know if I can stay forever, nor if I want to.

However, I know that I cannot make such a choice without him. I love him too deeply to cause him pain. "I would have followed you to the Earth realm as well, if I could."

"I know that, too." I pause, thinking of all those prayers I heard. I cannot hear them here no matter how hard I listen, but I'm beginning to hear whispers. They are not yet clear enough for me to hear the words that they are saying. If I listen long enough, perhaps I will be able to understand them. "There are not as many souls coming into the Underworld," I mention gently. "Is that because my mother and I did magic together?" I ask the question gently.

"Yes," Hades says with a sigh. It does not sound resigned. It sounds proud. "It was quite the thing to witness, Persephone, if only from the Underworld." My heart beats dully not wanting to think of my mother and her grief. When Olympus realizes I am gone, I don't know what they will do, but that knowledge is not for me at this moment.

"And…things are healing here as well."

"Now that you are here… I was not at my best in your absence."

Hecate told me about the destruction of souls… and about what had occurred while I was on Olympus.

There's a new tension between us as I choose my next words carefully, so I rub my fingertips along Hades's rough knuckles. Whatever he did, it is not something that will separate us forever. I will not let it be.

"You sent demons," I say, with my hand still over his. Hades's demons are one of the few ways he can influence the mortal realm with the powers he has here, and they are one of the main reasons so many mortals cried out to me in prayer. They were desperate for help. Most of them had not faced demons in generations and did not know what to do to save themselves. According to Hecate, they prayed to every god and goddess they could name. The fear struck them in the heart and caused delusions and harm in ways that cannot be undone.

"I had fears of my own," Hades admits. There is a small hint of defensiveness in his voice, but it is almost too quiet to hear. "As above, so below. As within, so without."

I turn in his embrace, pushing up off his chest and putting my hand to his cheek. I press a kiss to his lips before I pull back and look into his eyes. "My king, you are more noble than that."

He shakes his head, and I see it then—the pain in his eyes at what he did and how alone he felt. It is written there for me to see and to feel in my own heart.

"I know," I murmur and lean in to kiss him again. He seems to need more of this, so I climb into his lap and let him rest his hands on my waist. I drape my arms over his shoulders and kiss him as gently as I can to soothe the deep ache in him. He's hard underneath me, but we keep the sheet between us, and I stay on his lap without rocking into him, just giving him my presence. This is needed, too. "I know how much you hurt. I heard of how you suffered. I do not blame you."

"Don't you?" he asks, leaning his forehead against mine.

"No," I say softly. "One cannot be blamed for such pain. You reacted in the way you did, and I've heard of it, and now the Underworld is healing again. Whatever hurt you caused is not permanent."

"Some of it is."

"And you can make up for it. You can be the ruler of your realms. You can be the king I know you are."

"I would be any kind of king for you, my queen."

His words force my chest to ache in a way that I'm becoming too familiar with. This tortuous pull that rests in hopelessness. I keep that pain inside me, not saying a word about it, until Hades seems to be able to relax and let go of some of the guilt he feels. I don't think he should let go of it completely, nor do I think any ruler should—but he cannot suffer from it forever and let it corrupt him as a king. Afterall, the gods are flawed and it is in those flaws that balance lies.

He would never forgive himself.

I would forgive him, but he would not, and I cannot let that be his life.

We must move on from this. I do not wish to stay in this torment.

I pull back and put my hands on either side of his neck. He slides his hands from my wrists to my shoulders, then back down to my waist, watching me as he does.

"Tell me what you are thinking, my queen."

I take a deep breath.

"I…must go back." My throat tightens and I nearly choke on the admission. It hurts to say the words, but it will hurt more to pretend they are not true. We *must* be able to discuss this. The pomegranate seeds. The mortal realm. The duties I have to the mortals who dwell there. The duty to my mother. He must realize the pain it causes her and that she too would rather destroy her-self than live in that agony. "You know that, don't you?"

"You must stay," he answers coldly, both his hands tightening on my waist. "You know that. Don't you?" The air chills around me with his possessiveness.

I stare into his steely gaze, unable to make myself argue with him. My heart ticks, ticks, ticks. I know I must do both. I cannot see how I could choose one life over the other when they are both mine. It would mean abandoning one of the realms, and every time I think of that possibility, I'm sick to my stomach. The churning revolts inside of me.

Hades frowns as my thumb brushes over his lips. He has marks from my fingernails on his chest and shoul-ders. It would be much easier to lose myself to his kiss and his body than to have this conversation, but it is un-avoidable, just like the choice I must make.

"Do you not feel your power here?" he asks as he lifts one of his hands from my waist and brushes a lock of hair away from my face, tucking it behind my ear. "Do you not sense your belonging?" His question is a whis-pered hush; a deep crease forms between his brows.

Without my conscious permission, I release another breath, this one carrying both the sorrow I feel at being separated from Hades and the joy I feel at walking the paths here and having the power of the Underworld within me.

I don't know how to explain to him that I know it is a gift I have been given. My father should not have poisoned me with the wine. He should never have tried to make me into a mortal. But the absence of my powers taught me how valuable they are—in *every* form.

I crave it all. I am destined for it all. I know it so.

"I do belong here," I answer him, looking back into his eyes. I hope he can see how much conviction I have in the statement. I don't need to return to Olympus because I think the powers I have there are more worthy of my time. That is not the reason. "I have never felt more powerful than I do beside you."

He studies me, his expression a mix of sadness and pride and need and love. It's a very complicated expression, but I understand it without him having to explain.

Hades takes my face in one hand and strokes my cheek. "I have a gift for you."

"What?"

He reaches over to the table at the bedside, eases the drawer open, and takes something out.

It's a crown. With sharp obsidian points that reflect the light beautifully.

It's dark, and yet it shines in the light. There are black, crystalline jewels worked into the delicate palladium and brushed silver, and when Hades turns it in various directions to show me all its angles, I cannot catch my breath.

"For me?" I've never seen anything so beautiful. I've never seen anything that made me think it was *mine* with such a strong feeling other than Hades.

"For you, my queen."

Then he uses both hands to lift it up and set it on my head. As I close my eyes, it feels as if it belongs. With a spell, it binds to me.

I place my palms on Hades's chest, and he drops his hands and looks at me, his eyes moving from my face to the crown and back.

"How do I look?" I question with a simper.

His mouth curves in a smile that is filled with satisfaction. It fades slowly until he has never looked more serious.

"You look as if you were made to rule at my side," he says. "You look as if you could not possibly live anywhere but here. You belong here, Persephone. You look as if you are my queen and will never be anything else."

"I am," I say, my heart pounding. I mean it. I *am* his queen. But I am also my mother's daughter. I am also a goddess of life that many in the mortal realm pray to. They rely on me to bring life, and I rely on them to know where I stand as a goddess. "I will always be your queen."

Swallowing thickly, a new fear rises inside of me. I don't know if I will always be *here*, where Hades wants me. And I don't know what hell he'll unleash when I inevitably leave. Or whether or not he'll forgive my betrayal.

chapter 16

THERE'S A TREMBLING RAGE JUST BENEATH the surface. The surface of my skin, the surface of the Underworld, the surface of all of my existence. It's ominous and although I'm aware of it, I ignore the tremors out of fear of what I'll do next.

The one thing I crave the most is to stay in bed with my queen until she speaks the truth I need to hear: *she belongs here with me for all eternity. Only here and only with me.*

It is a great irony. If she hadn't come back, the Underworld would not have started to heal from my rage. If she hadn't done magic with her mother and said whatever it is she said to Demeter to stop the carnage on Earth, the previous rage would still be unleashed…and that is quite harmless compared to what resides within me now.

"We must go," Persephone tells me simply, pulling me from my thoughts, her arms around my waist. We stand in front of the mirror in my bedchambers. She is breathtaking in a black silk gown that gathers on the floor at her bare feet, the crown I gave her on her head, her hair in flowing natural curls over her pale shoulder. "The court is waiting for you." Her voice is a lullaby. It soothes the beast inside of me.

"They're waiting for us," I remind her, then turn away from the mirror and take her chin in my hand. Her skin is so soft, so delicate. The love I have for her feels as if it's on edge because of her admission: *I must go back.*

Persephone tips her face up to mine without hesitation, and I bend to kiss her without hesitation as well. The genuine affection soothes me. She is a balm to my broken soul.

Why would I ever hesitate? Why would I ever leave her unkissed? I would not. I will never again deny myself her love, however I may have it. I tell myself she's here now and she would not betray me. She would not leave me. Although something inside of me screams that she will. That it is destined. The pain in my chest is unbearable and yet, I stay beside her. I ignore it. I bury it deep within me until the screams are silenced. With that I deepen the kiss, losing myself in her touch. *Stay with me, my love.*

Persephone makes a small feminine sound and pulls back, breathless. The blush on her cheeks is tempting. "Hades! They're waiting!"

"Let them wait," I tell her, my voice low with lust, and I kiss her again. The warmth of her embrace is everything I need.

The next time I come up for air, Persephone whirls away. I catch her around the waist and pull her back toward me loosely, kissing the side of her neck playfully until she twists out of my arms with a huff of a laugh and hurries out of my rooms ahead of me. "We must," she urges and stops to wait for me. Not leaving my sight, which makes me grateful.

There are guards in the hall, of course, and the last time she was taken from the Underworld, I watched it happen and did not intervene. I allowed it. A foolish side of me under the spell of the Fates' promise allowed it. Never again. She knows not what it did to me. Never fucking again will I allow it.

In the hallway, Persephone loops her arm through mine with her other hand on my forearm and stays close to me while we walk, guards ahead of us and behind. Her hip brushes against me. As if she cannot part from me either. I focus on that. On her desire to be at my side. I sink into that gratitude and the pride she has of being the righteous queen she is.

"You know it would not stop me," I whisper by the shell of her ear.

"What would not stop you?"

"The guards. The daylight. Take your pick, my queen. None of it would stop me from having you here and now."

Persephone gasps, mockingly she questions, "You would let them watch?"

My tone lowers as I respond coldly, "They would not watch if they knew what was best for them."

"You could not punish them for watching if you chose to do such a thing."

A bark of laughter leaves me. The laugh catches the guards ahead of us as they share a glance. Perhaps even a subtle smile. I do not watch them for long. I am far more interested in watching the color deepen in Persephone's cheeks.

"Promise me you wouldn't," she demands, nudging me with her elbow.

"You have my word."

Persephone purses her lips. "I suppose I will have to trust you." The lightness between us is pleasing. I carry it with me as we walk, leaving behind whatever had come over me.

I lean down to speak into her ear again. "I would not punish them for watching. But they would not watch, either. You are their queen, and not one of my guards would look at you in a private moment unless you asked them to."

She is quiet for too long.

"Truthfully though, I don't care about the guards," I say into her ear, like this is the most salacious thing I could imagine. "I don't care who is watching. All I care about is you. Unless it bothered you."

Persephone meets my eyes.

"I don't care about who fucking sees us, Hades. Let them watch, so long as I have you." She does not know how strongly she draws me to her. Tipping her chin up like that is nearly too much. I want to guide her into an alcove, push up her gown, and fuck her until she falls asleep from sated exhaustion.

Desperation is unbecoming, I know.

"Careful, my queen," I tease and then allow her a gentle kiss in front of the guards.

It's been too long since I held court, and it's important to Persephone that I remain the ruler of my realms in more than name. That means passing judgments. That means hearing what the souls who dwell here would ask from me. Answering whatever questions they have with honesty and transparency.

The guards, donned in blackened iron armor with skeletal etchings and dark red capes the color of blood, pull open the wide doors before us, and we walk into the court.

Persephone stands taller as we make our way through those who have gathered for today's session. The room, grand as it is, is crowded, but it is silent. The crack of the doors closing and the armored boots of the guards clinking is all that can be heard. Anticipation and fear mingle in the air. A twinge of guilt at their fear stirs in the pit of my stomach. Surely, these souls do not think I would destroy them at court.

Do they?

I resign myself to the idea that they must. Their fear

is sickening. It troubles them to a maddening degree. I've sent demons to the mortal realm. Purely out of anger, I've torn souls apart in nearly every part of my realms to make space. I must show them that I will not lose my temper here. That court is still a place of fair consideration. I will stand as their righteous king, and they will come to trust me again elsewhere in my realms as well.

The whispers begin as Persephone turns to face them before taking her seat.

Gracefully, Persephone takes her seat next to me, and that is when it happens. The wave of souls kneeling begins at the front of the room and floods backward until every person there is on one knee, bowing their heads for my queen. The sight is chilling in the most delectable of ways.

They bow for *our* queen. The pride I feel is a sinful thing.

"Oh," Persephone whispers, and extends a raised hand to them, acknowledging the gesture. "You may rise," she says finally, her voice thick with emotion. Her wide beautiful eyes turn glassy, and I reach over to place my hand over her hand that rests on her lap. She's quick to turn it so we're palm to palm and she squeezes my hand in return.

"We will begin," I say, raising my voice so all can hear, and the gathered crowd shifts its weight. Souls rearrange themselves, shuffling on the spot. I wait for the doors to open and the first soul to be judged brought before us.

A few voices rise when the doors do not open.

They're only a little louder than whispers, and this time, they are questioning. A prickle slips down my spine. A knowing feeling. This is not the usual routine, but it cannot be. There was too much unrest while Persephone was gone. It will take some time for the various processes in the Underworld to rebalance themselves.

Although irritation runs through me, I do not give any sign that I find this unacceptable. I did not expect the first new soul to be brought in without a moment's delay.

Persephone tightens her hand in mine. She, too, knows that there is unbalance. Holding my hand a little tighter is the only move she makes.

Just as I am about to speak—to ask if there has been some delay—the doors to the court open.

It's not a single, new soul that is brought in, flanked by two guards. Swallowing thickly, my shoulders tense.

It is Hecate.

Once again, the entire court falls to one knee, heads bowed. Whispers of graciousness and love follow her path. Hecate extends her hands to the crowd as she comes to the dais where I sit with Persephone, bestowing blessings on the souls. The weariness in her eyes shows me she has not slept since she's done her bidding in the mortal realm. Leading the army of the dead to seek their retribution and to force closure for their souls that was not granted before their death. Her robe is tattered, graveyard dirt lines the hem of it. Once for every moon's passing, the great Titan does her work for the dead. And last night she must've brought hell on Earth given her state. Good for her.

Finally, Hecate reaches the dais. She turns to each of the guards who have accompanied her and thanks them, her steady voice loud enough to be heard at the back of the court. The guards retreat back to the doors.

"Hecate." Persephone rises from her throne with an affectionate smile and steps down to embrace her. Every eye in the room is on her, though no one has gotten to their feet. "I'm glad to see you here. Have you come to make a request? If you have, please be assured that my king and I will hear you."

My heart thunders. Of course it is the right thing to say, but where did Persephone learn these words? They are a clear demonstration that we have no qualms with Hecate. We are not at war with her. She is the goddess of cycles and balance. Accepting her, even in the darkness, even in the most violent of times, aids peace and hope. Which is surely what this court is after.

Hecate glances over Persephone's shoulder and inclines her head to me before she speaks.

"My queen," she says. "My queen. I thank you for your kind greetings. I have not come to make a request, but to give you notice of my comings and goings. I wish for you to be prepared."

"Prepared?" I question, that trembling rage turning to something else. Something I can finally place: fear. Every soul who is gathered for today's session will hear me, because they have all fallen silent. They want to hear every word, because they will leave this session and repeat what has happened all through my realms.

"Yes, my king," Hecate replies. "I come to you to tell you that I will return to Olympus tonight. The new moon is high and will fall shortly. Soon, the new crescent will light the skies. This is the way it has always been, and the way it will be. This is a sign of balance. There will be balance among the realms."

It's not quite a whisper that ripples through the crowd at these words. It is more of an energy. A shift of knowing. As if the souls here do not dare to react out loud but are unable to contain their excitement.

"There will be balance," Persephone replies with a solemn nod, and this time, the *vibration* is even more palpable. The souls cannot stay still. They sway slightly, even down on one knee. Every face turned toward mine shows the same desire—to turn toward the soul next to them and speak of what has happened. To whisper. Perhaps even to shout.

My hand curls into a fist on the arm of my throne. Balance. The word is a hiss in the back of my mind, and I can't help but to stare at my queen. Hecate has said so little and yet so much. It's nearly a threat.

Persephone embraces Hecate again. Then the two goddesses separate, and Hecate gives a shallow bow in my direction. She turns with her head held high and leaves, bestowing more blessings as she makes her way out of court.

When the doors have closed behind her, Persephone

comes up the steps of the dais and takes her seat beside me. She slides one of her hands under my fist and the other on top of it, holding my hand in both of hers.

The touch itself is reassuring. Persephone has seen my resistance to Hecate's message.

"We will begin," Persephone states, and the souls get to their feet. The very next moment, the doors open, and a single new soul enters, the same guards on either side. There is no hesitation now.

The crowd feels free to whisper and they do.

"I am your queen wherever I go," Persephone says as the guards lead the soul to the dais. "And you are my king."

"Wherever you go," I agree as I repeat her words, although I can't stop looking at her. *What deal has she made with Hecate?*

"And your love is stronger than any other emotion, even anger," she says, a little faster. The soul will arrive at the dais in a matter of moments. She is an older woman with light and thinning, shoulder-length hair. She appears dazed and unsure of where she is. I know that Persephone will be kind to her. "Is that still true?"

"Of course it is, my queen."

Persephone leans over and kisses my cheek. A quiet gasp whispers through the crowd and is quickly stifled. "The Underworld is healing. You are healing, too. All is as it should be."

I place my other hand over hers and look into her eyes. I do not have time to say all I wish to say and explain the anger and fear twisting inside me, held at bay by her hands on mine. I do not have time to tell her what it means that her touch is comforting in this way, and how I cannot be expected to live without it again. I do not have time to tell her that I know, I *know*, that the realms must be in balance or they must be destroyed.

"All will be balanced in time," I say instead.

Persephone nods, a private smile curving her lips. She squeezes my hand between both of hers.

Then, without letting go of my hand, as if it is natural to hold her king's hand while she pronounces judgment upon a soul, Persephone faces the woman who has arrived at the dais.

The guard announces the reason for the soul's unrest. The brutal manner in which it was ended brings tears to many. The fact that she ended it herself but was not in her right mind, too concerned with her children having enough food to eat and not wanting to eat herself. She sacrificed her soul, although the penalty for suicide is well known. She could not easily be placed, as she thought if she only ate a morsel, she could be with her family, and no one would perish. This is the consequence of Demeter's pain and withering of the crops. Mothers died to save their children. But for how long?

"Do not be worried," my queen says, her voice soft, as comforting and welcoming as a thick blanket after coming in from the cold. "You are meant to be here. You have found your way, and now there is only a short journey ahead of you."

"And…then what will I do?" the woman asks, staring up at Persephone with wide, agonized eyes.

"Rest," Persephone says, smiling. The warmth in her voice is not a performance. It's as real as the warmth in her hands. "You are able to rest now and with that rest, you will have abundance." She turns her attention to the guards. "She is noble, although she misjudged her actions. Please take her to the Elysium." Her verdict brings a murmur over the crowds. "Do you agree my king," she asks me and I do. With a nod, the woman is taken away and the courts continue.

chapter 17

HADES REMAINS SILENT FOR SEVERAL judgments. He doesn't pull his hand away from mine or give any sign that he wants me to let go, so I do not. The nervousness that runs through me feels misplaced. This is where I belong. I'm meant to be by his side. I pause for him to take the floor each time, but he simply nods to me.

I keep thinking he will signal to me that he wants to take over in passing the judgments, but he does not. Four of them go by. Five. Ten. My heart beats faster for a while, but I keep my hands around his and steady myself with his presence next to me.

The questions still come to my mind: am I ready for this? Am I prepared to judge souls after my absence? How will I know what to say, and where to send them?

But as every new soul answers, I find that I *do* know.

It's achingly obvious to me. I find that I only need to observe them, and then look inside myself for the answer.

And it is there, just as my powers are in the Underworld, and just as they are on Olympus.

Hecate's announcement was not a surprise. The new moon does not last long, and she follows its path in the sky to come and go from Olympus or wherever else she may venture to the Underworld. I knew she would come to me when it was time to go back. The crossroads are her home. And those who are lost find her there.

I didn't expect that she would come to court, and I don't know why she made her announcement publicly.

I'll have to ask Hades about the exchange but not until we are back in his rooms. His rage was palpable, although I've no idea why. Is there not peace between them?

Hades does not let it show on his face, although it is very clear to me. It radiates off him, and I do not know how to ease that feeling except through my touch.

Finally, Hades takes an audible breath and straightens. For hours, he sat tall and proud before me, so I did not think he could be taller or more commanding, but somehow he is. Relaxing my posture, I pause once the guard states the reason for judgment needed and I remain quiet.

Hades turns his hand in mine so his palm is up and I can lace our fingers together. Then, as he passes judgment on the next new soul, he squeezes my hand as if to say *you did well.*

I glow with that feeling through the rest of the session at court. I spend most of it watching the gathered souls. They spend their time watching me or watching Hades. This is yet another sign of how difficult things were when I was gone. Every soul who meets my eyes seems to crave reassurance that the worst is over. Fear lingers still.

I hope the worst has passed. And yet, I know not what has occurred in Olympus. I also do not know what Hecate will reveal to them. I didn't even get a chance to say goodbye to Beatrice. But surely they know I lawfully took my leave after my displeasure with my father. Now that leaves me only with acquiring Hades's blessing to leave with Hecate as I need to so I may continue my work on Olympus as well.

Court goes by quickly and slowly at the same time. I'm torn. The pieces of me that have missed my place here wish to return to Hades's rooms, or even out into the gardens, where we can wrap ourselves in each other and let the hours go by in pleasure.

I also wish to show the realms that their queen has not abandoned them, even if I must take my leave from the Underworld at times.

I must, I realize. I must be gone from time to time. I cannot abandon the mortals, either. I cannot abandon my mother. At the thought of her, my gaze drops and my heart pains. My mother's grief spreads and causes too much pain to others as well. That is the nature of grief, isn't it?

There *must* be a way to make sure everyone has what they need. There must be a way to bring lasting balance to the realms. I will find it.

Relief leaves with a heavy breath of mine when Hades dismisses the court and the doors at last close. There are no more souls to judge today. We have made it through the first session after the realm nearly collapsed.

He keeps his hand on the small of my back as we go to his rooms, guiding me with soft pressure to keep up the pace. It appears my king is just as anxious to be alone as I am.

I find myself needing his touch. His approval. His kisses and desire. As his hand slips lower, to the small of my ass, a measured moan of pleasure leaves my lips, and his heated gaze meets mine. Guards be damned, they witness the interaction.

The second the door shuts behind us, he pushes me up against the wall, takes my face in his hands, and kisses me with as much passion as I give him. I'm needy for his love and approval. Our desires force moans into the warm air between us. Hades slides his thigh between mine and runs his hands down my body. He rocks himself against my clit, relentlessly. The pleasure is everything and all I need. He doesn't stop; kissing, sucking, and rubbing against my clit until I cry out and come on his thigh, both of us still fully clothed.

Flushed and breathless, I stare into his dark eyes filled with nothing but lust. Before he can kiss me again, I drop to my knees and tear at his clothes until I've freed his thick cock, then run my tongue through the slit at his tip making him hiss. Smiling to myself with utter satisfaction, I close my lips around his shaft and take him into my mouth until I gag. The head of his cock presses against the back of my throat and I love it. The depravity and the deep need settle in the heat between my thighs.

Hades lets out a rough groan and braces himself against the door, thrusting his hips slowly into my mouth. I wrap my tongue around him and let him fuck my throat, tightening my lips whenever I can. It's not easy to take all of him. He fists the hair at the back of my head and eases himself deeper and deeper. My eyes sting and water with his thrusts and I fucking love it. I don't stop him. I revel at his desire to take me this way. I manage to draw a few more groans of pleasure from him before he comes, moaning my name.

His release is salty yet sweet, and all I can do is swallow.

It feels filthy and perfect. I have never felt more like a queen than on my knees throbbing with need for him to please me the same way.

Hades pulls me to my feet afterward and swipes the pad of his thumb over my bottom lip. He breathes heavily, his chiseled chest rising and falling with each labored breath.

Then he kisses me again, slower this time. Warmth flows down my shoulders with his gentleness. When he pulls back, he takes my hand and leads me to his grand bed. I direct my magic at the fire, and it jumps up in the grate. Flames lick up instantly and the power I feel is undeniable. The hearth's heat and light pour into the room, adding to what's already there. The sun is still in the sky, though the rays are getting longer. It will be evening soon, and then it will be night, and Hecate will leave the Underworld.

At that thought, my heart stutters. Thankfully, my love distracts me.

Hades sits on the edge of the bed, and it groans with his weight. He draws me in between his legs. He takes the crown carefully off my head, setting it aside on the table. Slowly, he bends down and gathers the hem of my gown in his hands. The teasingly slow pace only makes me want him more. He lifts it up over my head, then lets it hang over the foot of the bed.

He lifts my delicate silk undergarments away next, one by one until I stand naked before him. Then he takes me by the waist and guides me closer for a kiss. With his warm tongue, he licks my nipples, then sucks at them gently but firmly, then runs his thumbs over them until I'm shivering with desire. My head falls back and soft moans pour from me easily. My clit throbs with need. Barely able to stand the incoming threat of pleasure, I whisper his name as a plea. Only then does Hades slide his fingers between my legs and circle my clit with his thumb until I come undone once again. Every inch of my skin lit on fire with envy of whatever part of me has his attention.

Hades pins me between his legs, holding me as I

come down. His hands return to my waist. He drags his gaze all over my body, finally meeting my eyes.

"I do not wish to chain you," he states. Once again my heart skips in that way it did before. As if it's attempting to escape the very cage it's contained in.

Swallowing thickly, I let my weight rest in his hands. I'm still lightheaded, still weak-kneed with pleasure. I would have more of it, if Hades would give it to me. It is not night yet. Hecate has not come. I am certain that *I* will come many more times before she arrives.

"Perhaps I would enjoy the challenge," I tease, testing him.

Hades's face hardens, and his grip tightens on my waist. "Do not tempt me, Persephone. I cannot stand the pain of your absence."

"You cannot see past your own desires," I whisper.

"Perhaps I'm blinded by my love for you," he says in agreement. "Is that a sin?"

"Maybe not, but it cannot be at the death of innocent souls," I answer calmly. My heart thuds in my chest.

Cupping his chin, I look deeply into his eyes. My heart aches. I want to give in to him. I want to tell him I will stay, and I will never leave. I want to tell him I can live without half of myself, but I cannot. I cannot split myself in two.

"I need what I have in Olympus, my king." It's painful to say the words. It's painful to take a breath to say more. But if I have learned anything from Hades and all of this hell we've been through, it's that I must keep my own strength. I cannot give it up, or I will never have it back again. "And so does the world and so does my mother."

Hades swallows and turns his dark eyes on mine. He does not squeeze my waist, but his fingers caress me there as if he cannot bear the thought of letting me go. As if he wishes he had the heart to chain me for eternity.

"Your mother? Your mother's rage resulted in that woman's death. Her starvation! How can you return to her when she's the cause of all of this!" His agony is felt, but it is rash and reckless.

"I'm aware of what she's done, but that woman will live with abundance. I could have promised her I'd provide that for her children too," I start, my voice tightening and nearly cracking, "but I cannot do such things when I'm here. I can only truly bring justice to her and her family if I'm able to be just to myself as well." I swallow the emotions, my heart beating hard beside Hades's as my words register. His gaze drops, and the cords in his throat tighten as his jaw ticks. He knows I speak the truth and the woman deserved more than what was given. She should have had security that her children wouldn't follow the same fate and yet, because of Hades's unrelenting possession of me, I could not offer her that.

"You are needed here," he says roughly, and I know it has cost him to say this to me. I know he wishes he did not have to. "I need you."

"I know." I kiss his forehead, then both his cheeks, then his lips. "I know, my king. But I will leave with Hecate."

Hades growls into my shoulder. His breath is hot against my skin. "You only have powers because of me. Your father would have seen you turn mortal."

"You cannot take the moral high ground when you were a partner in that deal. I gave you grace that perhaps you didn't deserve. Do you not see how I suffer too?" I ask him genuinely. "How I feel as your queen, who you grip too tightly?"

He avoids my gaze, refusing to answer.

"I despise your affliction, my king. It troubles me."

"And yet you lie in my bed," he answers. The resentment is not nearly as evident as his pain. He wars with himself and it's obvious.

"Yes. I lie in your bed and in your arms because that's what I desire. It's what I want. You, my mother, my father are all so concerned with what you want. What about what I want?" I question.

"I cannot have you only two nights in a moon's cycle," he says, his voice strained. Hades's control slips, and it's as if I'm watching him descend into madness. The unfairness of what he *thinks* will happen makes my heart race. I want to defend him from that injustice just as I want to defend the souls of the Underworld from the injustice of having their world collapse. *More* than I want to defend the souls of the Underworld.

"There will be balance," I promise him. His hands clench on my waist, then release. He huffs out a breath into my shoulder. "Have faith in me."

Hades lifts his head, removes his crown, and looks

into my eyes. The depth of his pain lies in the darkness of his gaze.

He traces a hand from my waist along my side, his fingertips moving up until he brushes them gently over my cheekbone, then the point of my chin, then my nose. Finally, he cups his hand under my chin and pulls my face close for another soft kiss that gradually deepens until he's exploring me with his tongue, turning his head to get a closer angle, pushing into me until I'm leaning back in his arms.

Hades could kiss me down to the rug like this. He could stretch out over me and push himself inside me and make me shake and shudder and come all over his cock, and I would let him. I would beg for more.

I do not want to leave with Hecate, but if I do not leave now, I won't be able to for so long and I don't know what will happen in that time.

I want to stay here, in this bed, with my king and my lover. With the god who gives me both power and pleasure.

I clasp my hands behind his neck, but only to get closer to him. He would not let me fall. He spreads his hands on my back, holding me as he kisses me.

I try to memorize how it feels. His hands are so warm and strong. His thighs are so solid outside mine. I am pinned by him, kept still by him, and yet I am also safe here. Nothing can poison me or harm me here.

Hades pulls me upright, his mouth still on mine, and breaks the kiss gently.

"You—" he begins, then pauses for a breath. I push my fingers through his hair as he readjusts his hands. They go back to my waist, circling my hips. "You ate the seeds. It is binding."

He speaks harshly, as if he is angry, but there is a certain vulnerability in his eyes that I cannot ignore.

"Hades." I lean forward this time. I'm the one to push into his space. I lean my hips farther into the gap between his thighs, feeling the muscles tense around my legs, and put my mouth to his. I lick his bottom lip and explore into his mouth with my tongue. I hold his face in my hands and keep him where I want him so I can feel him there, and so he can feel me as I am—naked before him, in his rooms, away from any prying eyes. Here, I am only his lover. I belong to him fully. I need him to know that I belong to him fully in every realm, even if I have other responsibilities. *Know,* I think, and kiss him harder. *Know I belong to you. Remember how this feels. Remember that I'm coming back. Never doubt that I am coming back to you. I will not give you up.* "Hades, you will let me go," I whisper the spell like a siren. Just as I've seen Aphrodite do a thousand times before…

chapter 18

Hades

I CANNOT BE STILL WITHOUT HER EVEN THOUGH I feel numb. There's a cage around the beast inside of me. I'm not certain how it's come to this. The events of her departure are hazy. All I remember are her moans as she straddled me and gave me a pleasure that drugged me.

Sleep is difficult at the best of times. I could not fall asleep easily when I was alone in the dark for all those years. When I was a captive. One would think sleep would be an easy way to pass the time, but it was hard to come by and disoriented me more than it comforted me.

It's difficult to explain. Most beings, souls or otherwise, cannot understand what it's like to live without life for so many years. Without purpose or meaning or sensation. With only my thoughts of being trapped and alone forever more. One loses a sense of time. Time to sleep and time to wake blur into nothingness. One loses a sense of *whether* one is awake or asleep when there is no sunrise or sunset to track the time.

I watched her go.

It was like watching the best parts of me disappear out of the Underworld, leaving only that crack in the sky behind. Then that was gone, too. Without her, it feels like nothingness once again. Although there is so much. So much that requires my presence and authority.

I consulted with the guards. I walked with Minox in the halls. I sat at a table and ate, though I cannot remember what.

And then I came to my empty bedchambers.

Staring up at the ceiling, surrounded by her scent that lingers in the silk sheets, it seems as if I merely exist. The firelight is dim above me. I would like to pass some of the hours with sleep, but when she leaves, it is as if I am back in that prison again.

What will be here when I open my eyes?

Not my love, Persephone.

Closing my eyes, I attempt to let my mind quiet.

It fills itself with images of her. Persephone, sleeping on the pillow, her sweet curves tempting me. Persephone, placing the tip of her finger to a rosebush and making the roses black as night. Persephone, both her hands on mine at court. The memories of her are all-consuming, like a drug that makes me crave her all the more.

All I can think is that she is not here. All I can feel

is the emptiness of the bed. Tomorrow, when I walk the path, she will not be there, and I will be left with her empty throne next to mine. She will not hold my hand at court. She will not pass judgments.

"At least," I murmur out loud. "There is proof she was here. The Underworld is cleansed of ash."

Cerberus rises lazily from his spot on the rug by the fire and pads to me, then hops up onto the bed. It creaks as he comes to me. He nudges sleepily at me with three of his noses, circles on the blankets, and goes back to sleep.

He's certain she will return.

Or he is certain that I will be fine either way.

I'm envious of his certainty.

With time drifting by too slowly, I go out into the hall, motioning to the guards to tell them I do not need an escort. My feet take me to my andron.

I wave at the hearth, and a low fire burns up from the logs. This late in the night, I do not need much light. I do not even *need* the mirror. I do not *need*—

I do need her. Curse all the realms, *I need her*. I've not negotiated with Zeus about scrying, and most of my life has proved to me that no one is waiting for me to need their presence.

No one. Not even Persephone.

And still, I go across to the mirror.

Its surface is dark and opaque. For a minute, I stand a short distance away. The closeness of it is almost enough. I can endure this separation if I am in sight of the mirror.

It's not a connection with Persephone, but it makes such a connection possible.

The possibility is all I need. Would I beg Zeus to allow her access to his andron? Could I bribe or blackmail a servant to cast a spell upon the still waters of Persephone's garden so I may steal glimpses of her in Olympus like I did before?

With Demeter's rage and Zeus's knowledge of my betrayal, I know not what my next steps should be. I've already broken many laws of the gods and gotten away with it. To risk anything is to risk losing Persephone.

But I cannot leave it alone. I cannot stand here, staring at a black mirror, then go back to my rooms. So perhaps the possibility is *not* all I need. My heart beats higher into my throat, practically suffocating me. What would it hurt? I will not let the ache of Persephone's absence send me into another rage. I will not.

I'm only going to see.

With one hand reaching out to the mirror, I take two decisive steps toward it. After a moment, the black begins to clear, fading toward the edges until the glass reflects my andron and my face.

That is what I expected to see. The Underworld and me in it. There was no reason to hope for anything else.

I'm about to step back when the reflection shivers. My blood heats and thrums with anticipation. I can barely breathe as firelight appears first on the edge of the mirror. Firelight on white walls.

And then a chair. And then Persephone's face,

close to the mirror, leaning in with a wrap around her shoulders.

I cannot help the pull to my lips that brings an asymmetric smile.

"You are here, my queen." My voice is low and holds a tone of reverence.

Persephone whispers, "I did not think I could be so lucky as to wish my pull to you would bring you here."

I lean closer, gripping the frame, wishing it were larger. Wishing I could simply walk through it. "Do you not sleep?"

"Do *you* not sleep?" she questions back coyly, with a beautiful blush moving to her cheeks.

"I do not," I answer. "Not when you are away."

"You cannot stay awake until I return, my king."

"I can do whatever I please in my realms," I answer her, the hollowness of her absence once again growing in my chest.

Persephone offers me a soft laugh at my response, but then her expression turns serious. "Not anything you please."

My throat goes tight at the memory of what happened before. "Yes. Anything." That is what it means to rule the Underworld. My authority here is absolute. "But I will not do *anything*, my queen. The souls here will be well while you are gone."

She arches an eyebrow at me. "Will they?"

"Yes." *As long as you return. Return now, and I will swear whatever you ask. Anything.*

I will promise her anything she wants *now*. The urge to bargain is strong, but I force it down. Persephone is not the person I want to bargain with. Zeus? Demeter? I will negotiate with them. Fight with them, if I must.

Not my queen. I will give her anything and everything.

Persephone looks over her shoulder. "I cannot stay."

"Don't go."

"Think of me, my love?" she requests with a hand to the mirror. My own hand meets hers although there's nothing but a slick cold beneath my palm.

"Every moment."

She stares into the mirror, her eyes darting everywhere, as if she cannot stand to stop looking at my face.

"I wish I could touch you," she whispers. "Scrying is better than nothing, but—"

Persephone does not finish the sentence, but the look in her eyes is exactly what I feel. It is far, *far* better than nothing to be able to scry and see her face. But it is far less than having her here with me. It is nothing compared with the feeling of her skin under my palms or her mouth on mine.

"My queen," I say, just as she ends the connection between us.

Persephone in Olympus disappears, and I am left looking into my own face in the mirror.

And what I find there is not the man I thought I'd see.

The man looking back at me is desperate. *Lovesick.*

Gripping the mirror as if it will keep him alive or pull him out of hundreds of years' worth of imprisonment. He looks like he would fall to his knees at the feet of his goddess if it meant he could spend five more minutes in her presence.

I straighten, but it does not change anything. I look just as I did before.

Finally, I resort to leaving the mirror entirely. I get far enough away that the surface changes to black, and I spend the walk back to my rooms trying to rearrange my expression so that it is no different.

It's only when I close the door behind me, shed the clothes and shoes, and climb into bed—Cerberus has not moved—that I realize my expression must have shown my feelings for Persephone long before tonight.

How many times has she seen that expression on my face?

How many times have they *all* seen it? To know that she has changed me forever? That I would bend to her will?

A voice hisses at the back of my mind, *What does it matter?* I cannot change this feeling that has come over me. I will never change it. Persephone could spend the rest of her days on Olympus or in the mortal realm, and it would never change. And who the fuck are they to judge me?

I think of her in the mirror instead. Waiting for me. Hoping I would be there. Sitting there with the soft fabric of her robe around her shoulders. The delight in her eyes when she saw me. Her power is undeniable. She pulled me to her. Perhaps the Fates' warning for Zeus was right. She would grow to be more powerful than him.

The very thought forces that fear back. The reason that I do not wish her to ever leave me. She is a danger to Zeus. And he knows it.

He's already tried to kill her once and I do not know if he'll try again. A numbness grows through me until I fall asleep thinking about her.

The night passes quickly, though sleep does not ease my desperation for her. I wake up with the image of her in the mirror fresh in my mind.

She's all I can think about during the day's session at court. All I can think about as I walk the path with Cerberus.

She's what I am thinking of when Minox joins me on the path, sliding out of the shadows and falling into step with me.

"My Lord," he greets me and I reluctantly oblige. "Minox."

"I have no intention of repeating what happened last time, Minox," I say, after a minute.

"I knew you would not, my Lord."

"I promised Persephone they would be well."

He glances at me. "When will you go to Olympus, my Lord?"

Freezing, I stop on the path and stare at Minox. He stops as well and meets my gaze, his expression placid.

Only a flicker of emotion in his eyes gives away that he does not know how he has mis-stepped.

"What did you say?"

"I asked when you planned to go to Olympus."

"I cannot go to Olympus. You know that."

He inclines his head, agreeing. "You cannot freely go to Olympus."

"What do you mean, I cannot *freely* go to Olympus? Of course I cannot *freely* go to Olympus. That has always been the case."

He swallows thickly, perhaps doubting himself. "My Lord, forgive me. I thought this was a possibility you might have discussed with Hecate."

"Hecate." I practically whisper her name as Minox's suggestion races through my mind. I am damned and condemned, cursed and yet blessed to rule the Underworld. Day in and day out I must stay, for I am needed and the divine law requires each of the ruling gods to be bound to their territory. Zeus to Olympus and the mortal realm, Poseidon to the seas, and myself to the Underworld. Hecate, the keeper of the keys, knows this law well. She was present for its creation.

"Yes," Minox says slowly, concern in his eyes. "Hecate is bound to return to the Underworld for Diepnon, but she may travel freely between the realms during the hours and days around it. She prioritizes magic and such over law… It is perhaps a conversation…" he trails off.

With anxiousness racing through me and my mind whirling with the possibilities, I turn away from Minox and stride down the path. He waits only a moment before following me. Up ahead, Cerberus reappears on the path, a stick in his middle head's mouth. He tears toward me, proud of himself. I bend down and take the stick, then hurl it ahead. Cerberus goes after it, barking and barking.

Minox glides up next to me. "My Lord."

"I did not have such conversations with Hecate," I admit to him. I question Hecate's reception to such things. My heart pounds. "When Hecate was in the Underworld. That is not what we discussed."

"Ah," Minox says with a slight nod of understanding.

"There is no favor I will not ask of Hecate, or any god, Titan, or mortal, if it means I may have my queen by my side."

"Do you plan to discuss it with her then?"

"Gather those who may know where she is; tell Hecate I need to speak with her urgently. I will scry if she does not wish to return to the Underworld. I am amenable."

"Yes, my Lord," says Minox and glides away more quickly than he came. Though I cannot be sure I saw correctly, I believe there is a trace of a smile on his face as he goes.

chapter 19

THE DARKEST OF NIGHTS ALLOWED FOR ME TO creep about before any soul knew I'd returned. With the morning light, I prepare to see my mother first. Nervousness pricks the tips of my fingers. I imagine she realized I left of my own free will and that those who carry whispers from the Underworld to Olympus would tell her I sat by his side and ruled.

The soft breeze blows a stray hair from my face as I look out into the pale blue sky leading the way for the sunrise. My mother is not so easily seen from my rooms, but I can see her tending to a garden. Her sage robes are adorned with a wheat wreath. She grows poppies and plucks them into a wicker basket. I imagine the spell she wishes to cast knowing the properties of poppies. The color matters of course. And the deep red narrows it down. It won't be for sleep or dreams as those would be blue. Love, fertility, or a prophetic dream if she places them under her pillow.

My heart breaks wondering if it's a spell for me. If it is, I hope she knows her magic is powerful, but I'd always return to her without the pull of her spell.

"My queen!" Beatrice cries from behind me, startling me and pulling me from my thoughts. With a quiet gasp, she shuts the door to my rooms hastily behind her. "You have returned," she rushes the words out with disbelief.

"I have—" I swallow the lump in my throat and regain my composure. "I didn't plan to be long; I do wish I'd had more time and thought so I could have prepared you."

She bows her head, her hands clasped together and pressing against the cotton apron she wears over her simple cotton gown that falls to the floor. "All is well now that you are home," she responds with ease. When she lifts her gaze to me, I note the dark circles, and guilt rises once again for leaving in secret. I know she worried. So many left with questions. I will do everything in my power to never do that again.

"What can I prepare for you my lady? Tea, nectar, or wine?" she offers.

There isn't a thing I care to eat or drink until I've spoken to the one person who I'm certain I've hurt worse than Beatrice by leaving unannounced. "I saw my mother in the garden. Will she be in soon?"

"No." Beatrice's eyes go wide. Her fingers tug on one

another as she speaks. "She's been tending to the gardens since she discovered you were not here."

I give her an apologetic look and take her hand. "Is everything all right?"

"It is all right for the moment, but I cannot say it will remain that way for long."

"What happened when I was gone?" I swallow hard, guilt churning in my gut.

"Zeus spoke to your mother." Beatrice takes my hand and guides me to my changing room. The gown I wore to leave the Underworld will not be the one I wear to speak to my mother. Beatrice seems to understand that, because she begins helping me out of it. "It was a spectacle, both of them blaming each other. He convinced her to give you time." She lays the black gown aside and slips a clean robe over my head. It's blush in color and soft and elegant. "She has given orders not to disturb her."

"Yes," I agree, watching myself in the mirror, wishing I could find Hades yet again within mine rather than my father's scry. "I will rest a bit more, then. I certainly need it," I add and then take in a steadying breath.

"Do you need food? Drink?"

"Both please," I answer. My body hums with the change in scenery. It is like having a candle lit inside me. The powers I can access here carry a different sensation than those of the Underworld, and I notice it most when I have just arrived in either realm. It's heady. As if my magic misses me.

Beatrice slips out of my rooms and returns a moment

later with fruits and a honeyed nectar. I have both at the table and find myself tired and yawning as soon as I'm finished. I've been restless and it's showing.

Beatrice leaves me, and I climb into bed.

Tired as I am, I cannot sleep.

The early morning is quiet, with the waxing moon not yet a sliver still lingering. Even so, my mind will not quiet. I toss and turn for some time before I sit up and look toward the grate.

The mirror is still here. I stare into it imagining my love watching me. Maybe with my power growing I do not need to sneak to my father's scry. Maybe I can will this world to bend to my needs. Maybe…I dream.

With a gentle murmur, I wake, blinking away a sleep and a dream I can't quite remember. Beatrice is there when I wake. She helps me into my blush gown and settles the wreath of roses onto the crown of my head. She dresses me as the queen I am here, and when she is finished, I go out to meet my mother.

She's still in the garden. I cannot tell if she ever stopped tending to them.

"Mother," I speak to gain her attention.

My mother looks up, and her face is transformed by her shock. "*Persephone.*"

She rushes to me, accidentally kicking over the basket in doing so, and I hold out my arms for her embrace. If she is cross with me, it doesn't show. There is only love between us. There is only warmth. I watch her as she gets closer. This is my mother. There is so much love in her eyes. So much care for me. It has torn her heart out to think I was missing or stolen from her.

Our conversation will not be a confrontation, I decide. It will be a plea. I will ask her for this favor as a daughter asks a mother for a blessing. Although the very thought of it sours my stomach.

Her arms close around me, and she pulls me into a tight hug, her arms shaking. "Persephone," she whispers into my hair. "You were gone."

"I was," I tell her. "But I was fine, Mother. Please. Don't fear for me when I must go."

"You must *not* go," she utters but doesn't relent her grasp.

Her arms tighten around me even more. Instead of pulling away, I hold her back just as fiercely. This is what she needs from me. I will give it to her before I ask her for what I need.

And I *do* need it. I need for the realms to be balanced. I need for Hades to be reassured. I need for all the death and strife to end, and for my life to be…

Mine. I want my days and nights to be the life I desire, and the life I must have been destined to live. As queen of the Underworld and the goddess of life. Both are to be mine, she must understand.

When my mother shifts, I release her. Her hands linger on my upper arms for a moment, then she drops them to her sides. Her gaze looks over me as a mother does.

I offer her a hand again. "Come inside and talk to me, please."

My mother glances at my hand, then at my face. The sun rises higher above the garden walls, shining its light onto my mother's hair. Her eyes are red. She looks as if she hasn't slept, and she is thin, as if she has been forgetting to eat as well.

It is brutal, the guilt that I feel at this moment. Had I told her though, I don't believe she would have relented. I don't think her state would be changed.

That is always how my mother has been. When she focuses deeply on her plants and her tending, she puts all of herself into the work. Only this time, she is not focusing deeply on her plants. Not *only* on her plants rather.

She is focused on me, and where I will go, and if I will be taken from her.

That cannot be the way. I won't ever be taken again, my leave is my own doing.

"Come." I hold my hand out again and wait. At first I think there is a chance she'll refuse to speak with me about this. She may turn to her plants. She may say they need her. That she left them to seek revenge in the mortal realm, and now she must put things right. She may try to delay.

But then my mother lets out a soft sigh, brushes a lock of her hair away from her face, and puts her hand in mine.

"Tell me about the flowers," I request from her as we leave the garden. "Tell me what is about to bloom."

My mother obliges easily. If there's one thing she'll speak of at any time it is of harvest and florals. She tells me, her tone absent, as we walk the cool halls to my rooms. I draw my mother down to sit on a chaise with me and listen to more about the flowers in the garden beds. The flowers we might plant together. The ones she has already planted and has watered carefully, so that the gardens here will be properly balanced again.

With the mention of balance, I sit up straighter.

"Mother," I say, when she falls into silence. "That is what I want to talk to you about."

"The garden beds?" she whispers, nearly mocking me with her head tilted. Sadness still lingers in her gaze.

"Balance."

Her lower lip trembles. "Persephone. You cannot mean to leave me for the Underworld." Her words are a hushed whisper dosed in fear.

"Please listen," I start.

"I cannot hear you say goodbye for the last time."

"I won't." I'm quick to cut her off as tears threaten to spill from her tortured gaze. "What I mean is that the realms need balance." I look into her eyes, keeping my expression calm. "The souls in the Underworld cry out for it. The mortals on Earth cry out for it as well."

"There is already balance," she argues.

"But the realms will not be healed until there is true balance, Hecate has told me."

"What more do they need?" Her eyes narrow, and her face, which had cooled once we were out of the sun, goes pink. "I have not kept anything from the mortals this time, and you cannot accuse me of causing harm to the souls of the Underworld. They followed the path they were meant to take."

"Of course I do not, Mother. You could not have harmed any soul in the Underworld. You would not."

"I would not!" she cries, and I hold her hand until she catches her breath. "I would not," she says, softer, though we both know what she did when she could not find me. She *would* cause harm to the mortal realm. *Mothers would do unfathomable things for their daughters.* I know this to be true. I know, in my own heart, that I would do the same for a daughter of mine, and more. "What are you asking of me?" she questions.

As my throat tightens, I take a deep breath and meet her eyes. "Only that you let me go."

She waits for me to say more. When she realizes that is my only request, she blinks as if she is just waking up.

"Go to the Underworld?" she says, her voice wobbling between flat and breathless. "You know I will do anything to stop those who wish to take you to the Underworld to never be heard from again."

"No—that is not what I mean. I do not mean for you to let someone *take* me there. I am asking that you let me go there, to be—"

"To be with Hades?" She is horrified. I can see that in her eyes. "The man who stole you away?"

"Think about it, Mother. For a moment. The events

that unfolded. Think about what happened with the wine."

My mother's eyes go dark with anger. "If Zeus has poisoned you again…if he has poisoned your mind—"

"He hasn't," I say quickly, then reach for her hands once again. She's distraught and on edge. The trauma clouds her judgment. "Mother, he has not. But he *did*. He poisoned me. He tried to take my powers from me and make me into a mortal. That was not because of Hades. If it is anyone's fault that I was in that position, it was Zeus's."

"Then it is Zeus who should pay for what he has done!" My mother tries to stand, but I keep her with me. "It is Zeus who should suffer my wrath."

"He has power over this realm, and the gods and goddesses here. He has power over the mortal realm as well. He is god of the gods. But he did not destroy me and he cannot. He will not and he should know that now."

My mother softens, reaching out to stroke my hair. "Because you were born with such powers, Persephone. Because of the prophecy." My mother purses her lips. "That he would be eclipsed by one of his children. That they would grow stronger."

This realization seems to make time stop. Even my heart pauses beating. *Fear?* My father poisoned me out of fear of my powers? As if I would use them against him! I would never have done such a thing. I had no reason to think I was in danger on Olympus. I thought he would be disappointed to learn that I could not find the powers that had been foretold. I thought he would want more for me.

His fault is his ego. It always has been and always will be.

The realms will never be the same to me now. I saw my father as powerful, and he does indeed have power over the gods and goddesses of Olympus and over the mortals.

His powers have not protected him from his fears. He thinks one of his children will surpass him, and he cannot stand the thought.

It made him *poison* me.

The rage I thought I let go emerges once again, but I breathe deeply for the sake of my mother. "I am not his only child."

This, too, makes everything look different in my memory. I think of Athena saying *he only tries to kill his favorites* to my mother and wonder how many times he has plotted against his children. If he plots against *all* of us. If he fears all of us because we might one day discover that we have powers he cannot dream of.

For how could he dream of something new when he spends all his time watching to see if one of his children is stronger?

I am stronger. I have never poisoned someone innocent out of fear. I never would. I have surpassed him already. If Zeus stood in the courts, I would suffer great difficulty sentencing him.

"But you are one of the most powerful," my mother says, and drops her hands back to me. "You are *my* daughter, Persephone. And whether you have powers or not—"

"I have them. I found them."

"I know it. But they are not the most important part of you. I would fight for you if you were a mere mortal. I will fight for you no matter what." The softness disappears from her face, replaced by determination. "If what you desire is to dwell in the Underworld, then I cannot prevent you from going there. But if you are away from me where I cannot reach you, there will be consequences. My grief will be felt and I cannot help it, my child. In the times you are away from me, the mortal realm will feel the loss. I cannot and will not change that for that loss is too real and too significant to be ignored."

chapter 20

Hades

THERE IS TROUBLE IN THE SKIES ABOVE THE Underworld.

From the towers, the flashes of lightning strike one after the other. There's no answering roll of thunder, and at first I think I am only imagining them—but no, they are there, splitting the morning colors. The cracks are bright and only last for a moment. They are not of Zeus's power.

Cerberus runs to my side, carrying a stick in the mouth of his left head. I take it and toss it for him, then watch him dart around the grounds to find it. He stops for a minute and barks at the sky with all three heads, then peers at me.

"Cerberus," I call, and he comes. I take him with me as I walk the path, surveying my realms. It is calm for now. New souls are arriving, although many are holding fear of demons or suffering from the pain of those in-flicted by them. I have already sat in judgment of them this morning. The meadows and fields are quiet, but not empty. I cannot remove the demons I've unleashed, the mortal realm will remember she was taken from me and the pain I felt for all eternity. Such is the ways of gods and mortals.

Another flash of lightning hits the pale blue sky, forc-ing it to darken. Chills run down my spine as I think of my love.

Up ahead, Minox slips out from a shadowy part of the forest, looks in both directions, and hurries toward me. He does not run, but he moves with an urgency that is unusual for Minox.

"Minox," I call as soon as he is close enough to hear. "What is it?"

"My Lord." Minox is slightly out of breath as he ap-proaches. "I have news of Olympus."

My blood turns hot as I command, "Come with me."

We return to my rooms. I will not have this news delivered where any souls may be privy to hear the gos-sip of gods. The peace in my realms is fragile enough as it is. They do not need to concern themselves with what the gods are doing on Olympus.

"Tell me," I demand, as soon as the door to my cham-bers is shut.

"There is to be a meeting of the gods and goddesses," Minox informs me. He steadied himself on the much-faster trip back to my private rooms, Cerberus racing ahead of us, caught up in my urgency. Now the dog is at the window. "On Olympus. About the trouble in the realms."

I raise an eyebrow. "Has Demeter called this meeting?"

He shakes his head. "Zeus."

"And I am supposed to sit here and wait for word? *Persephone* is on Olympus. My queen is there."

"My Lord—"

I hold up a hand to silence Minox. It's not just news from Olympus I have been waiting for. "Have you heard from Hecate?" I am bound to the Underworld. Physically incapable of leaving. The golden threads tie me to this place, and I've never felt like a prisoner until I laid eyes on Persephone.

"Not yet, my Lord. But I will try—"

Minox is interrupted by a thunderous *crack* from outside. It splits the sky in two violently. Cerberus barks before howling and his call is joined by two hounds.

My body is paralyzed by the sight of a dark cloud dissipating, and in its wake a cloaked figure lit by a torch. *Hecate is here.*

The guards open the heavy audience room doors as Minox and I make haste to our guest.

A servant brings a tray of fruits, a pitcher of water, and a cask of wine. Hecate sits at the head of the table, her hooded cape draped around neck while both water and wine are poured, then lifts her wine glass to her lips. The wine brings color to her cheeks and lips. The Titan's face turns younger. The mother, the maiden, the crone. The three faces of a woman's life fade into youth. The maiden. Surely, she thinks of Persephone as we enter.

"Ah," she says when she puts it down, a small smile on her face. "I am refreshed." As I pull the heavy wooden chair out beside her, the legs scrape against the floor. The servants line the room, but Minox requests their leave before leaving himself and shutting the doors so we may have privacy.

"Hecate. Thank you for coming." She grants me a modest nod before admitting, "I saw that you would ask me to come."

"Do you know what is happening on Olympus?" I question, the nerves caused by my queen's absence still rattling in me.

"Sit, Hades." Hecate gestures with her glass. When I do not sit, she gives me a look. "Sit down. We must talk."

I take my seat although I'm restless.

Hecate sips her wine again, then gracefully reaches for a piece of cheese with honey and a single ripe berry on the silver tray between us. Her eyes close as she enjoys the decadence of the meal. I do not reach for anything. I don't plan on indulging in the meal until she gives me another look, as if it is somehow rude not to eat when Zeus is making plans and calling meetings on Olympus and I am here, without Persephone.

Begrudgingly, I take a morsel. The doors open and a servant enters with a decanter.

"At your request," she states and I motion for her to come in.

It takes a century to summon a servant and wait for wine to be poured. The taste of it on my tongue reminds me of Persephone. She tasted the wine, then when I returned from court, she kissed me, in those days when she was beginning to blossom. I would much rather be drinking with her.

Hecate thanks the servant and lifts her drink, all the while I imagine what may be happening on Olympus. A trial perhaps? The clock ticks as Hecate keeps me waiting. She exhales, finally seeming satisfied.

"You and I had an understanding," Hecate begins. "We both knew of Zeus's habits."

"I did not betray you."

"You had Persephone taken from her rooms in the middle of the night rather than waiting for her to be nearly mortal. So much so that Zeus would remove her from Olympus. How is that not a betrayal of our agreement?"

"Our agreement was to bring her to the Underworld when the danger to her was too great. Doing so was not a betrayal."

She stares at me, unmoving. Hecate knew of Zeus's actions and the deal I conjured with him. "It was to be me, Hades. She was to come with me at the new moon so that I could offer reassurances to Demeter, and

Persephone could choose to be with you. Your impatience is your demise."

"Yes." I burn with the same anger I did when Zeus informed me that he would make her mortal. I never wanted her harmed. I only wanted her mine. "It *was*. That is what we agreed on. It is Zeus you should be angry with."

"He moves against all his children," Hecate counters. "This is nothing new."

"He was the one who wanted her out of Olympus and reached out to me to begin with. Either way, it was *Zeus* who demanded she go. And if I had not—" I am not the same as I was that night. I had to stand in front of the mirror until I could hide how I felt. Now I know it is impossible. I cannot hide how I feel. Not even from Hecate. "If I had not taken her that evening, I do not know what would have happened or what she would have become."

Hecate runs her finger along the edge of her wine glass and stares into the dark red pool. It was wine that Zeus used to poison Persephone. The rage and fear I felt that night mix into a deadly concoction. Perhaps I went around them all to attain my queen. But it is Zeus who bears the consequence, not I.

"Well, then." Hecate places her glass carefully on the table, then lifts a sweet from the tray and eats it. I find my hands clenched on the table in front of me and unclench them as Hecate chews and swallows with a thoughtful expression on her face. "You had no choice. You *had* to take her." Her tone is mocking and I grit my teeth.

"I had to send Minox. I could not take her myself, as you know." The admission stings. "There was no time to summon you and—"

"Was there not?"

My jaw ticks as her face morphs into the crone and then back. She is a knowing Titan. "There may have been time to summon you," I admit. "But it was not the new moon, or even close to it. You would not have been able to come."

"You are mistaken." Hecate leans back in her chair and it creaks with her movement, her wine drawn close to her chest. "It is not only at the time of the new moon that I may move between the realms as I will it."

"But you are bound—"

"I am *bound* to return to the Underworld at the crescent before the new moon. I may travel between the realms when I wish. There is no other binding, and you are aware of such things."

With a deep breath I steady myself. My instincts war with me and my muscles coil. I want to knock the dishes off the table. I want to hurl my glass of wine at the wall and watch it shatter. I don't; I restrain myself. Something it appears I've been doing more often lately.

"It was not my intention to betray you," I say, when my vision clears. "I was mistaken and for that you have my apologies."

"You might have asked, Hades." Her tone is gentle but even still, it enrages me.

There is no reply to that beyond a scream of frustration. Surely she knows what was at stake. The Titan is the oldest god. She's walked through fires that burned centuries before I was conceived.

The respect I have for her is only outweighed by the knowledge that she is the key to Olympus that I need. I do not let my rage out. I stare across the table at Hecate instead.

And Hecate, for all she is willing to sit here at this table with me—for all she did come to the Underworld at my request—will not understand what it is like to ask a question of your own mind and get a twisted answer back, then come to believe it when there are no other voices and no other people.

"I wanted her and I did what I had to in order to take her," I admit coolly.

"Who opened the realm?" she questions.

"Aphrodite, at my offer to reunite a demon soul with his fated love. I took advantage. I implore you not to disclose this indiscretion." I answer her honestly, praying that she will be willing to forgive all if only I am honest.

"I suppose you thought that you could not wait," she muses, as if she can see into my mind. "I suppose you questioned whether I would betray you to Zeus the moment I left Persephone with you. I suppose you thought there was truly no other choice."

I give her a nod of agreement and do not utter a

single word. That is all I can do. To open my mouth and explain is entirely too dangerous. Once I started, I might not stop, and then Hecate would be privileged to have knowledge about me that she would never forget.

"Yet," she continues, "you have asked me to meet with you, because part of you hopes that I may be able to offer you passage to Olympus."

Her guess is correct. "That seems to be something you are able to do," I force out. "If there is to be a meeting of the gods and goddesses, I wish to be there too."

Her gaze drops and then rises again with a heavy breath. "You wish to be there with your queen," Hecate says quietly.

"Yes."

A smile curves her lips. "Persephone has changed you after all. You would not have come to me before you had her as your queen."

I swallow thickly. Yet again I am at the mercy of others and I loathe it.

"Love changes a man," Hecate says, as if she is only thinking of it now. "Even if he does not know it himself."

Straightening in my seat, I clear my throat. Hecate has had her conversation. She has seen too much of me, and it is knowledge I cannot take back from her. I'm not willing to give her more—not until I am by Persephone's side.

If I can be at her side, then I will give Hecate anything she asks.

Given the satisfaction echoed in her eyes, I think she knows it.

"I am asking you to grant me access to Olympus so that I may attend this meeting along with all the other gods and goddesses. Will you allow it?"

Hecate places her wine glass on the table and stands with a flourish. She holds out her hand, still wearing that unsettling smile, as if she was the one who set all this in motion. As if she was the one to guide my fate.

"Let us go to Olympus then, my Lord," Hecate says easily. "Why ever did it take you so long to ask?"

chapter 21

"WE WILL DISCUSS IT," ZEUS ARGUES WITH a hiss. His arm rests on his throne as if he is exhausted by my questions. The gray sky darkens more until it's lit with flashes of irritation. As if the sky above admits he's at his very limit and can take no more. As if the daughter we share and what he did to her is of no importance. "You must have patience, Demeter."

"I *have* had patience. I waited for her to return, just as you wished. And what does she say?" My heart rages inside of me. She is a piece of my soul. She is mine to protect and provide for.

He closes his eyes. My disgust and anger trembles the ground beneath my feet although I try to contain it. It is impossible to reign in grief. It is poison. One all will know the taste of.

"She says that she wishes for me to let her go to the Underworld. *Live* in the Underworld. How am I to dwell here for eternity, knowing she is as good as dead!"

"Then perhaps, Demeter—"

"Do not *say* I should let her! Do not say I should allow this to happen! What standing do you have to say such a thing to me when you do not offer consequences for those who took her? It is because you aided such deception and you know it!" My throat is hoarse from my screams and accusations. Even with the tremors beneath us, he is unmoved.

Zeus looks out at the light beyond the throne hall and considers the skyline as if it might give him answers. When has the sky ever done that? It is always Zeus, alone in his rooms or with whatever nymph is in his bed, who decides whether the sun will rise and set.

Zeus is a god with so much power that he has forgotten what it means to exist with others. He is only concerned with making all the realms bend to his ego, with no threats to his power. Every god who exists has their own magic, and within it the possibility of having more power than any other. It merely depends on the time and situation.

I'm just as much of a fool as anyone else who has gone to his bed. I thought our daughter would be the exception.

I thought Zeus would have seen the gift she is and understood that she has always been more concerned with the mortals who pray to her. Persephone did not want his throne. She is not like Athena, a strategist of war. She is brave and beautiful in her own way, but she was not a threat, he turned her into one. He forced her into that role. This is his fault! There's nothing but frustration in ruling over other gods, who fight and plot against each other, and who will do so for all eternity. Gods never change their ways!

And here is Zeus, sitting on his throne, the same as he ever was, telling me to be *patient*. Telling me to let her go.

It would be safer for him, no doubt. It would make him feel more comfortable if his daughter wasn't here to remind him that she still exists and now she's more powerful than he could have ever known she'd be. All his doing. Irony is a lost art form.

"Do you have an answer?" I demand, stalking closer to his throne. My fingers stretch before me and then ball into a fist as I walk forward. It's an attempt to keep the magic at bay. To ease the build-up of agony so it may not burst into rage and disaster. "What standing do you have? Who are you to make this decision for her? For *me*?"

"I am—"

"It does not matter what you say!" I cut him off in a hiss. "You *have* no standing! There's no one in *any* realm who would agree that you have the right to betray me and your daughter as you have!"

"I am god of the gods, and I have done wrong," he says and his voice is barely raised. He glanced at me, sullen, playing with his beard like he has only just discovered it is there. "I only *weakened*—"

"And what was the point? What was the goal? It wasn't only to weaken her! It was to send her to the Underworld dead—"

"The mortal realm, first," Zeus corrects. Rage heats my blood. *How dare he! Was I to say goodbye to her, powerless as she aged in my arms?* The very idea forces my throat to close and my shoulders to hunch in sorrow.

"The mortal realm!" I shout at him. I've long lost any desire to be composed. The last months have taken from me any pride I ever owned. "You wished to send her to the mortal realm. Who was to be next? Me? What other gods do you fear so much that you must sneak poison into the wine?"

"No one," Zeus answers, his voice going soft but with a tinge of warning. That is the sign of *his* anger getting the better of him. Good. Be angry. Allow this war to truly begin. "And I will make the same argument to you, Demeter. *You* do not have the right to decide for all the realms that they should suffer and die. *You* cannot destroy the mortal realm and throw all the realms out of balance. *You* are not the only one who dwells here, either."

"I know I am not. I hear the prayers of the mortals and answer them, unlike you, who only hears prayers and people when they are convenient."

He rises from his throne. "If only I were free to focus on the mortal realm," he shoots back. "If only I had that kind of leeway, to leave this realm behind and lavish all my attention—"

"Is this really about *that?*" Zeus. A god with such powers. Such influence! He sits on a throne in the grandest halls on Olympus. "Surely you will not complain that I didn't pay you enough attention after you were finished with me!"

"That, Demeter, is where you are mistaken." He moves toward me, pointing, his face red with fury. "I was not finished with you then. I *am* finished with you now. I will not have—"

"Your daughter alive and well?" I snap.

"I will *not* have the realms in chaos. I will not have you causing havoc in the mortal realm and disturbing all the other gods. I will not have Hades raging in the Underworld over *one*—"

"Do *not!*" I point into his face as well. "Do not say that Persephone is only a girl! Only a daughter! She is greater than you will ever be!"

The sky cracks with lightning as Zeus raises his voice.

"She will be *nothing* if this does not end. I will make it so, Demeter. Mark my words, I will—"

"You'll do what?" I press him. "What justice do you offer when you're responsible. Does it irk you so that you've given her more power by attempting to snuff her magic out?"

The sound of the unfamiliar voice raises from behind us and a chill runs through me. Zeus and I both turn at once. This voice is not one that can be found on Olympus. Never. He has never set foot on Olympus before.

It is not possible. A depth of coldness paralyzes me as my eyes land on the tall dark figure. His black crown sharp and the tips lit with fire.

There is Hades, with Hecate at his side, standing at the threshold. My heart breaks with the vision of Hecate. How could she allow this? The sight of Hades, though, consumes my attention; he reminds me of what Zeus did to her. Her capture in the dead of night. *Justice must be granted.* The lone truth whispers in the back of my tormented mind.

Athena focuses her attention on Zeus as I'm distracted. "You are threatening her again?" she calls, her voice clear. More faces crowd the edge of the hall. More gods. More goddesses. Many of those who dwell on Olympus. Those who will bear witness. The whispers and murmurs fill the space as I suffocate staring at Hades, his dark eyes meeting mine.

"That is not the way we settle things," Athena continues. "That is not the way we *will* settle this matter, or it will never end."

"I do not think it needs to come to this." Aphrodite follows Athena, offering a soothing gesture. Others come behind her. While Athena makes her way to Zeus, Aphrodite comes to me and takes my hands. "Demeter, please. No harm came to Persephone, in the end. It was a game, really—"

I snatch my hands away. "It was no game."

"You do not need to seek revenge. Not when she is at peace. You do not need to keep her locked away—"

"I am not the one who has *ever* locked my daughter away! She was not a prisoner here when her father gave her poisoned wine!" I'm blinded by his betrayal. All this time while I grieved, he knew. He fucking knew.

Hades's black boots crunch on the ground as he stops at the threshold. Hecate removes the hood of her cloak unveiling the vision of the crone. Her wisdom brought her here. Bought them here. I swallow thickly, barely contained. I remind myself of what lies in my pocket. A potent dust of poisonous poppies. The wind would carry it for me. The deep sleep it would cause would haunt the gods' dreams with their faults. Every memory they regret would play over and over again for centuries until they woke. My fingertips itch to simply allow it, but my gaze is caught by Hecate.

"Do you see the contradiction?" Hades states, his voice carrying past Aphrodite. "You demand that she stay here, never returning to me, though this is where the greatest threat to her life dwells? You want her to stay with the god who poisoned her? Who wanted her mortal, or better yet *dead?*"

"I need her with *me,*" I snap at him. "That is something you will never understand." My gaze flicks between Hades and Hecate in front of me, and now Zeus is at my back. I stalk toward the edge, Aphrodite's hand in mine as she pulls me from the center of the room so that the parties may be separated but see one another. Zeus at the throne, Hades by the entrance, and me at the edge of the hall.

And so war has come to me. Perhaps all I needed truly was patience.

"I *do* understand Demeter," Hades tells me and it's a lie! He cannot understand this pain. A crowd forms around Hades. A circle of spectators lies at the edge of our circle. These matters, hearings of sorts are never truly private—not on Olympus. And all the gods and goddesses will take a side. I hear their whispers. That I was crazed. Oh the looks on their faces though when they learned of Zeus's betrayal. Was I not right to be crazed? Driven mad by deceit and loss.

Some of the crowd only want to drive those who argue into a hotter frenzy, as a sport. Some of them have an eye toward their own children and their own futures. Some of them want Zeus's favor. Others want my favor so I may bless them with abundance. Whispers spread from the threshold, as well. *Hades* is here, they call to those who chose not to come. How could they resist such a spectacle. *Hades has come from the Underworld to steal Persephone away again.*

My hand stretches yet again at the thought, and I can imagine blowing the fine red powder in his direction. Hades himself moves toward me, glancing at Zeus as he does.

Come closer, you fool. Breathing heavily, I wait. I

allow him to move freely. Come to me so that I may end this once and for all.

"I knew not what a sickness love was until I loved Persephone. She is all I think about; all I want. The pain her absence causes me is one that is worse than all of the hells I could manage. No, Demeter, she is not a daughter to me. She is my *queen*. And every day in the Underworld is torture without her."

"Then you wish for us *all* to live in hell." These men will drive me to madness. They cannot look past themselves. They cannot see what grief they are capable of causing, even when it is laid out in front of them. It is far too much to bear. "You wish for the Underworld to be here. You wish for the destruction of this place, and when Olympus has fallen, you wish for the mortal world to fall as well." Murmurs rise within the space as fear flows freely.

Hades shakes his head and raises his voice for all to hear. "I do not want every realm to be the Underworld. I only wish to rule my realm with my queen beside me where she belongs. It is known. She is now the queen of the dead. I only wish to be granted what is demanded by law and not condemned to an eternity in hell. She took my hand in union, she ate the seeds that bind her to the Underworld. And yet, you claim I have no right to her presence. You attempt to keep me from her!"

Seething with rage, I cannot trust myself to speak at his accusation.

"And where does that leave us?" Zeus shouts, rising

from his throne and pushing his way closer. Both men coming closer. I stay as still as can be. The Fates blessing me with a possibility I could not have dreamed of. Both of them at once, suffering the spell I hold in my pocket. "Where does that leave *my* realm and all the gods and goddesses in it? Do you think your precious Underworld would still stand without our work?"

A few voices rise to agree with Zeus. The two gods are too far away but as they posture and tensions rise, they grow closer and closer together, closer to me as well.

Come closer, I will. At the thought, Hecate's eyes catch mine and my heart races. *Do not interfere with my justice, witch!*

Hades ignores the voices, carrying on about balance and Olympus's rule being the one true law. He narrows his eyes at Zeus. "If I were you, Zeus, I would be far more concerned about my own status."

Casting my gaze out to where the gasps come from, I realize more gods and goddesses gather around. I would not be surprised if all of Olympus was here. Hermes and Eros peek from the corner, arrows at the ready. My heart races. Would they take aim at me if I were to do what I came here to do? I had not thought past my intention. Aphrodite reaches out for one of my hands, but does not take it. She is too struck watching the argument come to a head. Athena, too, has been swept aside by Zeus, but she leans around him, staring at Hades.

"Do you mean to declare war?" Athena breathes

with narrowed eyes. More curious than angered. "Do you mean to fight Zeus for control of Olympus?"

"No," Hades scoffs. "I meant to remind him—and *all* the gods and goddesses of Olympus—that if all of the mortal realm were condemned to the Underworld, there will be no one left to pray to you. Your existence would be futile."

"If you take her back there," I say quickly, before Zeus can bluster on again. "That is what will happen! The mortal world will not know life! There will be no new harvest. The mortals will die by the thousands."

"That is what *you* would have as well," Hades replies. "You are the goddess who went down to destroy the harvest. Is it the company of your daughter you want, or is it truly to have the mortal world as your hostage?"

"How dare you!" In a blinding rage I spear Hecate with my gaze. "There are those among us who knew where Persephone was taken and hid this from me. Who were they loyal to, I wonder? Was it Zeus, with his poison? Was it Hades, with his demons? What promises have been made in secret, when no one was listening? How many plans have they made against all of us, and we were only meant to suffer with no recoil?"

The faces of the other gods turn toward me. Their eyes flicker over Hades and Zeus and Hecate. They sneak glances at those around them. Discontented whispers rise in volume.

My heart races, and my stomach turns. It is sour

from stirring up this kind of suspicion. It is not the way I prefer to exist in any realm.

I do not wish to turn the gods who bear witness of Olympus against each other, but I do not see what other choice I have.

Zeus announces, "I will defend Olympus as I always have."

"You must!" Athena cries beside him. Her elegance only shaken slightly. "Or we are all caught in a web of lies and deception! We will defend ourselves! There is no threat you can make that holds ground, Hades!"

"Hades is the outsider," another goddess cries—I cannot see who. "Send him back to his realm before he drags us all there with him."

"I will not leave without my queen," Hades says. "And—"

Thunder strikes beside us as Zeus throws a lightning bolt.

It does not hit Hades, but crashes into the floor, leaving a large, burned crack in the shining marble. The smell of ash hits me with a force as the rubble crumbles.

Hades narrows his eyes, arms wide with a blazing fire in his palms.

Chaos erupts. Gods and goddesses turn on each other, running away for safety and pushing past one another. Powers crackle and sizzle through the air. Aphrodite pushes me to the side, attempting to save me from harm's way? I cannot tell what she is doing.

A cloud of smoke rolls across the room, obscuring the others from me.

In the back of my mind, my vision obscured from the smoke, I hear Hecate's voice so clearly. *Blow it now if you will, and all will live in their regrets within a deep slumber, including you. If you are too weak, I can do it for you,* the dark goddess offers. With smoke burning my eyes, I envision the turmoil I ensued. The pain that ripped from my palms as I starved those who called out to me for mercy. Tears prick my eyes.

In the corner of my eyes flames burn hot higher and higher.

"No," I answer, coughing on the smoke. It chokes me. "Stop. This is not—this cannot be the way—"

It's all spiraling out of control. This was not what I had planned.

"Stop this," a booming voice commands, cutting through the screaming assaults, calm and strong. "Stop this now!"

chapter 22

"STOP THIS NOW!" THE VOICE THAT RISES FROM my throat is one of spite and detest. This fight does not have to do with me. Rid my name from it. It is the anger of their chains and their discontent with fate that causes them to rage against one another. My chest rises with a hollowness that's undeniable. I cannot stop this war if they continue to believe it steeps from my taking my new place as queen of the dead.

No, that is not what this war is about.

The chaos of the gods and goddesses of Olympus is like nothing I've ever seen.

The gods, in my father's great hall, attacking one another—

It fills my lungs with the need to scream. Viciously and violently. The vibrations and power in the courts could call a thousand years' worth of life. It could build and rebuild Olympus, even if Olympus itself were thrown to the ground in the mortal realm and left to crumble into ash.

Olympus does not fall underneath this power. It shudders and shakes. Holes appear in the walls and the ceiling, letting the thunderous rain through, soaking all who stand here. Beatrice holds tight to my hand.

"My lady," she says into my ear. "I told you it was not safe. My queen. We must go. We must leave this place. This is a matter of the gods—"

"I am the goddess of life and the queen of the dead," I argue back, not looking at her. I search for any glimpse I can get of Hades. There he is, throwing shadow-demons out ahead of him. They fight off the gods who join my father's army and attack Hades. My heart tumbles with fear. There is my mother, her hand on Aphrodite's wrist, the two of them facing out into the fray. There is another one of my father's lightning bolts. It's maddening. All of this pain, for what?

It all happens in slow motion.

I attempt to step forward, but Beatrice pulls me back. "My lady, please—it is too dangerous. Let us retreat to somewhere safe, and then we can pray—"

"To whom?" I ask, searching her gaze for an answer. "All the gods are here. They are *fighting*. It is not the time for prayers, Beatrice."

"You cannot fight!"

"I will not."

"But my queen—"

A bolt of power—a lightning bolt, perhaps, though I cannot see exactly what it is—slams into the corner behind Beatrice. It cracks and shatters the stone that's been there for centuries.

"Enough!" I pull her with me into the hall, step up onto a fallen fragment of the ceiling. I draw my power from every being. Their life is my source.

With my eyes pitch black, my robes a haunted ash, and no crown atop my head, I raise my hands, my fingers bent and twisted as vines creep from the ground, winding around limbs and holding those who fight in place. Screeches cry out as the vines twist and slowly silence the slaughter.

I've never felt so powerful and I command once again, "Enough!"

My voice carries out over all the gods of Olympus who have gathered here to argue and attack. Over the bloodied attacks and screams of rage.

It takes a moment for the movement to stop, the screams to be silenced by the vines, but it does. Those not contained by my hold slow as the realization of what I've done dawns.

"There will be no war in my name!" I shout and know it to be true. There is no doubt that I will put an end to this madness. As my power moves away from me, along with my words, I see it reach each god. One by one. Stilling them just as the binds grip them.

Thorns grow at the throats of those who struggle.

"Be still!" I command as the magic flows through me more easily than it ever has.

My father stops. He's visible in the center of the crowd, large and brooding, his staff in his right hand and his gold crown ever shining. He watches me with wariness in his eyes. Bolts of lightning strike down at the vines that grow near him and yet, only more grow in the injured plants' place. The more he fights, the more power he gives me. I watch the flash in his eyes as the realization dawns on him. It is then and only then that his staff is held close to his chest and his attacks are halted. "Stop at once!" he booms. "It has ended!"

My mother, a short distance away, clutches Aphrodite's hand. Regret pure in her gaze. Hecate, on the other side of the hall, has her hands folded in front of her, head bowed and her hood covering her face as if she has not been in the middle of a battle. She stands as a statue murmuring incantations.

The only person who moves, then, is Hades. He steps out from behind a small gathering of other gods trapped within the binding vines and into the light. His broad shoulders rise as he breathes heavily, and then I watch as he flexes his fingers and pulls the shadows of demons within him back from whence they came. His gaze is narrowed and pained. A single slash across his face, no doubt caused by my father. I turn my attention to each of them. My mother, my lover, and my father before slowly releasing the vines.

"Persephone," Hades whispers and I'm drawn to him. The tension crackles when I meet his darkened eyes.

Within the depths of his gaze lies pride and loyalty. But mostly love and admiration. He is looking upon someone that is *his* and only his. Someone whom he will gladly defend for as long as he's capable of living. He bows his head as he whispers, "My dark queen."

I find him fair and just and certain—though not perfect. But even his imperfections are known and accepted in the Underworld. His wrongs can be made up for and forgiven.

Beatrice squeezes my hand, pulling me from my thoughts of my lover.

"No more," I say clearly as the ash and dust settle. I do not have to speak loudly for my voice to be heard at the other end of the hall. "There will be no more fighting."

There is shuffling as the gods and goddesses of Olympus tuck away their arms. Metal slides on sheaths. Bows land on backs, held there by the finest leather straps. More than a few knives, glimmering with layers of added power, flash in the air as they are put away.

"There will be no more fighting on my behalf in Olympus," I proclaim, as if it is a prophecy I have heard. Let it be so. I know I am stronger in will and love than my father, but whether I am truly more *powerful* does not matter. All that matters is if my father *thinks* I am. And more than that—if he thinks I am like him. If he believes, with all the powers I have found within me, I will end him if he chooses this war…then the war will never be. Whispers grow in the crowd, a few scuffles are heard behind me, but I do not turn. I stay where I am. My mother to my left, father to my right, and Hades ahead of me. All others slowly back away.

"I will choose my own fate," I state, before the murmurs become shouts. "I do not wish for this *but*—"

The court has fallen silent again. A prickling grows over my skin with every pair of eyes on me. They are all watching, and my heart thumps faster.

It's then I realize, I'm not afraid. I've sat on a throne built only for me at Hades's side and looked upon tortured souls in the Underworld. I've passed judgment on them, granting them rest or punishment. I've seen my word carried out without question, with those souls and everyone in attendance watching. The difference this time is that I am not passing judgment on others. I have looked into my own soul and made a judgment for myself.

In the silence, they wait for me. Wait for me to speak. Wait for me to tell them how this story will end.

My mother, even my father, hold still with bated breath.

"It is known that all the realms are connected. If one realm suffers an imbalance, the other realms will follow." My father opens his mouth to argue. "This is true. We have seen it already, and none of us wish to see it again. We must follow the divine law."

"Tell us, Persephone," Aphrodite calls. She has both my mother's hands in hers now and guides her toward me, her eyes flicking between my mother and my father. Aphrodite keeps them moving until they are level with Hades. I do not know if my mother knows this. She has not taken her eyes off me. "What balance can there be when hearts are torn?" Her knowing eyes reach mine.

I reach into the pocket of my gown and take out the six seeds I have kept with me since Hades tipped them into my hand. Six eaten and six remaining. Half and half. I have moved them from gown to gown, counting and re-counting them, making sure they were with me always. They have been my prized possessions, and now I know why they are so valuable.

"Hades." I speak his name and a faint light comes to his eyes. "You gave me a dozen seeds, one for each cycle of the moon throughout the year. I have eaten six."

The crowd murmurs among themselves once again— to demand to know more, I think—but I hold up my hand to silence them.

They fall silent.

My mother whimpers, a frown marring her face, and I can barely meet her gaze. Instead I focus on my lover. Who will bend the worlds' wills for me. Who will rip the binds of the Underworld to be with me in council.

"My Lord, king of the dead and ruler of the Underworld." I dip my chin but keep my eyes on Hades. "Of the twelve moon cycles of the year, we shall have six together." My voice nearly cracks at my decision. I did not know it until I spoke. My mother's gasp is chilling, but I continue. "For six cycles, I will stay with you."

My mother lets out a cry that is not a word. It is only a sound of sorrow and betrayal.

"Mother." I meet her eyes next although doing so forces tears to my eyes. "For the remaining six cycles, I will be here with you."

"You do not understand daughter, I cannot contain my grief. For the time you are away, it will be felt by all. The spell cannot be undone. The plants will wither and a coldness will settle in all the lands. It is only when you return, that life will break through the cold hard ground and begin again. My suffering…perhaps my suffering…" Her expression is pained. She reaches into her pocket, and her eyes widen with shock. Her hand reveals nothing and she pulls in the pocket before staring daggers at Hecate, whose cloak has turned to a vibrant red. My mother's dismay is evident, and I am left with more questions than answers. I do not understand what the two share in this moment.

"What is wrong?" I beg of her. "Please see reason."

"I cannot help what I feel. I love you too deeply. You are a part of my soul and it feels as if it's perished when you are there, in the land of the dead." She heaves in a breath. "For every moment that I am without you, there will be death on Earth. The suffering I feel when we are apart will be felt by all."

I allow her this moment but merely nod in understanding. It is still what must be. Over the whispers of the crowd, I solidify my decision. "Then when I am with you mother, the earth will celebrate and rejoice with life anew. And when I am with Hades, it will wither. That is the cycle of life is it not?" I turn to Hecate who merely watches. "We will bring seasons to the mortal realm, ones they may survive as well as endure."

I turn toward my father. "Is this just, god of gods?"

The crowd's attention turns to him, and he only nods in agreement.

With a small cry, my mother leans against Aphrodite, who pats her shoulder and whispers something into her ear.

"There is no need to fight for me," I continue, as my mother's grief spreads throughout the room. "No reason to keep the realms in a state of confusion and chaos. No reason for gods and goddess to turn on one another. This is my choice. This is my will. You have all witnessed it here with your own eyes. I have duties and responsibilities to the mortals on Earth, and I will see to them." I meet Hades's gaze as I speak that truth. "I also have duties and responsibilities to the souls in the Underworld as their queen. This way, I will meet them all and will abandon no one. I will be with my king half the year. I will be with my mother the other half. The time will be equal, and so will the seasons be on Earth. A season of growth and a season of honoring the dead."

"I will have access to scry with my love then," Hades states and yet it is a question directed at my father.

"It will be arranged," he answers easily. With that Hades relents.

"And so it will be," I finish, and lower my hand.

All the realms seem to hold their breath.

There is not a sound in the room. I swallow my fear that all that I have said will not be enough. That the gods and goddesses will disagree, dooming the realms to centuries of pain and death.

But then my father lifts his chin. "And so it will be," he says, sealing this promise. Making it a sealed law.

The rest of the gods and goddesses follow his word.

And so it will be. Although all three of them stare at me with unanswered questions.

"It is done." My father's statement ends the courts, but it does not at all feel like an ending.

chapter 23

A S THE ADRENALINE OF WHAT HAD OCCURRED earlier subsides, I sit with my own decision. Six moon phases will be the longest I've ever spent away and I won't be able to leave. And yet I remind myself, the time will go far too quickly when it is spent as we do.

Beatrice sits with me in my rooms, both of us before my altar. She takes a shaky breath next to me, audible in the quiet, and I reach for her hand.

"I'm not going forever," I remind her. "Half of the year, and then I will be back."

"It seems so…final," she admits, glancing at me out of the corner of her eye then lifting her free hand to wipe her teary eyes. "You, in the Underworld…"

"I have already been there, Beatrice. It was not so different from being here."

"Yes, it *was*," she says, turning her head to look me in the eyes. "You are sure you will not be lonely?"

I have to stifle an internal laugh at that. "No, I won't be lonely. I won't be alone for even a moment, if I don't want to be. I don't think Hades will want me to be alone, either." My stomach sinks at the thought of my king. How does he consider my judgment?

With a heavy exhale, Beatrice relents. "All right. *If* you won't be lonely."

"I've told you about Silvie. She'll be there with me as well. And—in case I haven't said, Beatrice—Silvie reminds me of you."

"Does she?" Beatrice's brow raises as does the pitch in her voice. "And that is a comfort to you?"

"Yes. She's knowledgeable about magic and the powers in the Underworld. She taught me many things about finding my own power. My own strength." The memories are fond although we didn't meet in ideal circumstances. "And she is always very patient with me, even when I take a long time to understand what she is advising me about magic."

Beatrice gives me a wry smile. "Allow the possibility of magic working."

"You are right," I tell her and tip my chin down, looking at the altar before us. We simply must allow it, fighting the magic is cumbersome and only gets in our way.

Certain aspects of my altar are the same as before. There is the large crystal I use for an energy source. There is the candle. These are other items I will use to cast the spell from herbs to oils.

But I will not be doing so alone. I will have Beatrice. We will cast together. I am not hiding away in the dark, hoping no one will see me trying to magic my powers to life and doubting whether they will work. I'll not be stolen away just as the light fills the room…

I only had time to kiss Hades once before Hecate took him to the Underworld. We did not have time to speak. We did not have time to plan. It is a taste, I suppose, of what some parts of the future will be like. Our time will be limited, and we must make the most of it.

"I'll watch over her," Beatrice says softly. "Your mother. If you would like me to do so."

"I would." A heaviness that I had not known was there disappears from my shoulders. "I…think she will understand, in time. But I know those months will seem to pass slowly."

"But not for you?"

"No. Not for me," I say with a sigh. "He is my king and I love him, all of him."

"You do truly?"

"I do," I tell her and let the smile show fully on my face. "I've found who I was meant to be at his side, and he…he sees me. He sees all of me. Even the pieces of me I thought might not be there at all. And the parts of me that I was ashamed of, he loved fully."

"Oh," Beatrice says, sounding slightly breathless. "You *do* love him."

My voice cracks with a half laugh. "How could you tell?"

"You're blushing." She traces her knuckles briefly over my cheek, a gesture that speaks to the closeness we have shared for years of my life. "And your eyes are bright. It was—forgive me, my queen. It was so long that the light in your eyes was…" Beatrice's gaze softens. "It was not gone, but it was dimmed. I could see the worry in your heart, but I did not know how to fix it. And I wanted to. I wanted you to be happy." She smiles, brushing a few tears from the corners of her eyes. "Now I see you are."

"I am," I reassure her. "I'm…excited, as well. Nervous. I will miss you when I am in the Underworld. I will think of you often."

"I will think of you every day, my queen."

I lean over and wrap my arms around Beatrice's shoulders. She hugs me back.

I take a deep breath, memorizing how it feels to be close to Beatrice, then release her. We share a smile, wiping tears from each other's eyes, then face the altar again.

"We came to do magic," I say, teasing her. "Not to cry. This is not a goodbye at all. I'm not leaving yet, and when I do, I'll be back in the blink of an eye."

"It will be a little longer than that, my queen." Beatrice pats my hand, then folds her hands in her lap. "But you're right. We came here to send blessings through the realm to sustain us all while you are gone, not feel sorry for ourselves."

Beatrice places her hands on the base of the candle. I reach out, mirroring her, and place my hands on the center stone, a large pale blue raw chunk of angelite. For peace and calm and centering one's soul. We will cast together, two halves of the same whole, the power flowing from the crystal to the candle and then out to the realms. I will offer up the power I can feel on Olympus, and guide it through those realms with my sense of the powers I gained in the Underworld.

That is the hope.

That is what *will* happen. I sit up straighter, breathe in, and then let it out. Next to me, Beatrice does the same. My arms tingle with anticipation.

This time, I am not asking for power on my own behalf, but for all the realms.

I close my eyes, the crystal warming under my fingers.

"The divine is within me," I state, and it is true. I do not doubt it. I do not have to try. I can feel it within me and all around me. "The divine is within me and with me, and I can bring light to the darkness."

I have done it before. I can do it again.

"Protect the realms from all that would wish them harm. Olympus. The mortal realms. The Underworld. Heal them from the strife that they have felt and smooth away the imbalances between them. Protect them from anything that would trouble them again. Guide the realms, and the gods and mortals within them, and the souls in the Underworld, to safety."

Beatrice's steady breath is calming beside me. She'll be gathering her sense of the moment as well. The sense of her powers. They are not as strong as mine, but they can still bring light to the darkness. Anyone can. All it takes is knowing you have a light inside of you. Our powers will mingle together as we do this, and our combined intention will send this protection throughout the realms.

"I release all that ails the realms," I say, and a sense of tension lifts away from my shoulders. A shiver runs through me, joining the warmth that is already growing in my chest. "I release it along with all that ailed me, and my father, and my mother. There is nothing between us that will stand in the way of balance in the realms. My powers are warmest within me. I send the balance I have found within my magic to the realms. It shall be there no matter where I dwell, burning like a candle that will not go out."

"Oh," Beatrice says softly. I will not forget this, either. I will not forget how much more powerful it feels to wish safety and balance on the realms, not just myself. If I find myself afraid again, I will remember to look outward. Beyond myself. Because I am a part of these realms, just as the other gods and goddesses are. Just as the mortals are. Just as the souls in the Underworld are. And using my magic to help them will also help me.

There's a moment of quiet. Beatrice waits beside me.

I take one more breath.

"The power inside of me craves the light," I say, and

Beatrice says it along with me, each word matching mine. Our voices just above a whisper. "Bring me the warmth of fire and take from the powers to my right."

The heat warms my palm. It is the heat of my powers and my blessings and the heat of all the powers swirling around us. Olympus is a place of great power, and there is much of it here, concentrated near my altar, where I have spent so long praying and trying to sustain my powers. It is still here. *I* am still here, and I will be back.

Because that is the way of balance.

That is the way of the realms.

That is the way of my king and of my mother.

That is my way. A way of balance. Of life and of the Underworld. Of love and passion.

"The power inside of me craves the light," I say again, Beatrice with me. "Bring me the warmth of fire and take from the powers to my right."

"The power inside of me craves the light." We speak with one voice, casting together. This will not be the only time we do magic. This will not be the only time we use our powers for the good of the realms. We will return to this place, again and again. It is only the beginning. "Bring me the warmth of fire and take from the powers to my right."

The casting of the spell takes my breath away. My powers feel like water, rushing through me and out to every realm.

It will burn bright until I return.

chapter 24

ONE KISS.

It is not enough and yet, I allow it to linger because it must be.

Eventually, I get to my feet and wander farther into my bedchambers. They're as empty as they were before Hecate granted me passage to Olympus.

My fingers slip against the ancient wood, and the memories of Persephone's time here are drawn to me. The images offer me a sense of peace I desperately need. I take the seat Persephone prefers, looking out the windows over my realms. Nothing tempts me in her absence. I don't feel like eating. I don't feel like drinking wine.

Cerberus circles the room, then comes to lay his heads on my leg. I stroke one head absently, wishing my heart would stop aching for Persephone. She'll return.

I will choose.

She looked at me when she made her wishes clear. The pride and acceptance of her judgment was nearly as consuming as my love for her.

In those minutes, it was as if there was no one else in that hall. We could have been in bed, Persephone leaning over me to kiss my cheek. Her words felt like they were mine and mine alone.

Half of them are. I let out a frustrated sigh, and Cerberus lifts his head, reminding me that he's here.

"I could not forget you," I tell him. "I would have liked to have you with me on Olympus."

Six months of this out of the year. Of every year. Half of all of my life I will be apart from her. I swallow thickly, understanding her decision and her duties apart from ruling by my side. The pain of her absence does not relent though.

What will I do?

I attempt to remember the days before I had her with me, and it's nearly impossible. The memories themselves aren't very clear. Did I just exist from day to day, doing the things I needed to do, with only the balance of the realm to distract me?

That must have been how I lived.

She won't find that acceptable.

My queen will never want to hear that I have spent six months worrying about her and isolating myself.

"What does she think I'll do, hmm?" I ask Cerberus. "Go on days-long walks with you?"

He hears *walk* and runs toward the door.

I stand to follow him, only to find the door opening and Minox gliding through. "My Lord," he says, a hint of surprise in his voice. "You have returned."

"I have," I agree with a sense of humor. "All is well in the realms."

"Is it?" he questions with slight shock in his tone and folds his hands in front of him. This is one of his oldest habits. "You seem…pleased, my Lord."

"My queen will be here six months out of every twelve," I tell him in a falsely contented tone. I desire all twelve months. I will have time to come to terms with it, however. I will have eternity to spend with my queen, even if I have to be patient. The realms will believe we are on a united front in this decision. They must not know my displeasure. My pain is for me to hold alone. "She will spend the other six months with her mother so that no one needs to fight over her. The realms will be returned to balance."

"They're much improved already, my Lord."

"To what cause?"

"A spell cast down." Minox's eyes brighten. "A spell from our queen. One to sustain us and heal what needed to be healed. Her whispers were heard by many who prayed for peace. Her magic crossed all the realms."

"The news makes me miss her greatly," I start and then correct myself. Perhaps Minox will be the only soul who has knowledge of my longing for her. "It pleases me also."

Minox hesitates. His lips part but he doesn't speak, withdrawing whatever thought he had.

"What is it, Minox?"

"Are you truly content with her decision?" he questions. "I suppose my fear is wondering whether or not her decision will last or whether you will make an alternative judgment?"

A beat passes and I know one truth. I would never fail my queen. *Never*. She needs this from me and the torturing I feel now will make my love for her stronger.

"She is my queen," I tell Minox, looking straight into his eyes. "I will give her everything she desires and more. This judgment will last, Minox. I swear it."

chapter 25

Persephone

I SPEND THE REMAINING WEEKS ON OLYMPUS with my mother. The mortals will now know true seasons and prepare for life as they should so they may have abundance in all ways. It is a balance that it is new for us all. But a beautiful balance indeed. In the fall there is slow death followed by a brutal winter. In the spring, life returns and then flourishes.

The season seems to stretch. The green spring is slow to turn to summer, but once it does, the summer days linger. Sunrise comes early, and the days are long and hot. Many evenings, when I scry with Hades, I do so in the light of the sunset, not needing a fire at all.

I crave him every minute. Every hour. Every day. I desire to lie in bed with him and feel his lips against mine. Even more, I want to fall into pleasure with him. I am lonely for it, and so is he.

When he looks at me through the mirror, it is with longing in his gaze. He leans his hand on the frame and touches the glass, and I can tell he would give anything to cup my face.

I place my fingers to the mirror, too. I would give anything to twine our fingers together. Even to feel his warmth through the glass.

But I cannot, so I become very good at imagining it is there.

The days are long with much work to distract me, so many have heard whispers of my name and the prayers are constant. But the nights, when I lay awake in my bed, are consumed with my thoughts of Hades and my need for him. I am at peace with my judgment, and still I long for him.

So I have been waiting for six long months when my last night on Olympus arrives, and I wake to my last day on Olympus. When the sun sets and the moon rises, I will go back to the Underworld, accompanied by Hecate, the keeper of the keys, and there I will spend six cycles of the moon with Hades.

I wake knowing that it is time. The summer is coming to an end, and the auburn colors of the leaves warn the mortals to prepare for change. The people may miss the long days, but they will welcome the longer nights and the chance to spend their evenings gathered close to the fire and go to bed early.

Six moon cycles, I think as I sit at my breakfast, eating a piece of bread with honey. There will be bread and honey in the Underworld, but it will not be the same.

Nothing will be exactly the same. That is part of the joy of going to the Underworld, and also part of the sorrow. I *will* miss things on Olympus. I will think of them with fondness.

But I will have my king.

"My queen," Beatrice whispers, coming through the door of my rooms. I greet her with a solemn nod. Our time to part is nearly here.

There is very little to pack. I will take a few items with me, but the gowns I wear in the Underworld will be there waiting for me. I will carry only a few keep-sakes with me.

My throat tightens as I place a carved crystal of a rose my mother gifted me the day after I made my judgment. It's made of garnet and the color reminds me of the pomegranate seeds, yet the flower reminds me of my mother's love. I put it out of my mind. Beatrice and I will walk in the garden and have tea. We will talk about magic and practice together. Then she will go, and I will have my evening meal with my mother. The sun has been setting earlier recently, so I know it is almost time to begin the next series of moon cycles. Tonight, the crescent before the new moon will rise sooner than it has in past cycles, and then…

Then I will go.

That is how the days have passed. A walk in the

garden where I appreciate every petal and the intoxicating scent. I cast blessings on Olympus and the mortal realm, and even bless my travel to come. Last-minute prayers to Hecate to thank her for connecting the realms that I may have both my king and my mother.

I am ravenous for Hades. And…I feel trepidation at the thought of leaving my mother for six moon cycles. I know I will be all right. I will be well and happy and fulfilled with Hades, but I worry for her.

She is quiet through our meal together. The silver's clinking and scraping against one another. We linger over sweets afterward, wine goblets in hand, until finally it is time to admit that the sun has set.

My mother keeps track of the moonrise out the window. There is not much to see with the new moon, but she can feel it. I know she will feel it every time it rises and sets while I am gone. She will be counting the days we are apart.

"Hecate will be here," I say, putting down my glass. I gather my belongings, then go to my mother and wrap my arms around her. "Be well," I say into her ear. "Do not worry for me."

"I will worry for you, my daughter," she answers, hugging me tighter. "That is what all mothers do. You cannot stop us." She gives me another squeeze. "Endings are also beginnings," my mother murmurs. "The Earth will rest, then grow again."

"It will be in balance," I say easily and note my mother's calm.

"The stars have aligned themselves, Persephone." My mother pulls back and looks into my eyes. She smooths a lock of hair back from my face and smiles, though I can see tears collecting in her eyes. She blinks them away for me. "My pain will be felt and shared but so will my hope and longing for your return."

"It is a beginning," I remind her, as she has just reminded me. "Please do not spend the next six moon cycles fretting about me."

"It is what—"

"Promise me you won't." I take her hand and squeeze. "Promise me you will scry with me, and you will plan for the summer, and you will take it as a time to slow down and sit by the fire."

"I may sit by the fire any time I want," she says, her brow furrowing.

"More in the autumn," I say. "Promise me."

My mother kisses my cheek. "I promise."

There is a loud *crack*, like the sky splitting open. My mother gives me one last kiss on the cheek, then straightens up. She looks proud, as the mortal mothers did on Earth when their children grew up and moved into their own homes. They were always so proud for their children to take their places in life.

I hope my mother knows that I have already taken mine. That part of my place in life is here, with her.

If she does not know now, she will know in the spring.

"Hecate is here," she says and swallows a lump in her throat. She releases me and closes her eyes, whispering and fighting back emotions. "Go to your king."

chapter 26

Hades

"Hades."

I am prepared for Minox, so Persephone's voice sets my heart racing. Fucking finally. Every nerve ending in me lights aflame and my breath is stolen from me. Finally, my queen returns. I whirl around as Cerberus leaps from my side. My dog is the first to reach my queen, and Persephone bends down, her travel satchel slipping from her shoulder and falling with a faint thud.

She's breathtaking in a blush pink silk robe with floral pin in her hair.

"Hello," she says, ruffling whichever of Cerberus's heads she can reach. The dog barks a few more times, then runs around Persephone and out into the hall. Announcing her arrival and racing to tell all of the Underworld, our queen is here.

She's so beautiful and the air around her bends to her power. Her return is a soothing balm to my soul. That is her scent in the air. That is her gown, and her face, and her sweet lips.

I am with her before I realize I have taken a single step. Cupping her face, I tilt her chin up for a kiss. She's *here*. This is not a dream. Persephone looks up at me, her hands coming up to cover mine, and smiles a gorgeous and lust-filled smile. She is sinful with what she does to every inch of my being.

"My love," she says in a low voice. "I'm here."

I lean down and kiss her once again.

She tastes of honey and sweetness and love. I moan into our kiss, and she presses herself closer to me, deepening the embrace. Persephone wraps her arms around my neck and pulls me down. Her warmth consumes me. Barely paying attention and without breaking our kiss, I guide us to the bed chambers until I can slam the door shut with one hand, then throw magic at it to lock it. Parting my hand from her lower back was torturous and I'm eager to reclaim her curves. We cannot be disturbed.

My cock has ached for her for months, and now that she is in my hands again, I will lose my mind if I do not have her.

"Hades," Persephone gasps in a sweet moan against my lips. It's evident she needs me as much as I need her. Our movements are not graceful as we tear apart the clothing we wear. It's painful to stop kissing her, but I must. I need her gown on the floor. I need to see all of her, every inch of her skin, so that I know she is well, and she is here, and she is *mine*. I strip her clothes over her head like I *have* lost my mind and let them drop to the floor until she is naked.

Then I sink to my knees. Worshipping every inch of her. *Mine.*

Persephone leans against the door, her cheeks flushed and her chest heaving with her breath. "I missed you very much," she murmurs.

"You have no idea," I practically groan in response.

I take one of her knees in my hand and pull her leg over my shoulder, then pull her close and take a languid lick of her. Her head falls back and her fingers find my hair. She cries out my name as I suck gently and prepare my queen for the ruthless fuck she's about to receive.

Persephone moans above me and my mind is filled with her. There's nothing else. Only her sweet folds, already wet for me, and the taste of her, and the arousal that I've craved and starved for. I did not forget her. I did not forget any part of her. She's familiar on my tongue, but I devour her pussy like this is my last chance. I press my tongue over her clit and make circles until she comes, letting her weight rest on me. Her hips surge forward into my face, which is a demand for more.

I give it to her.

I give it to her again and again. Climbing the highest of highs with her chest and cheeks flushed until she falls down begging me for more.

She's still leaning against the door when I add my

fingers and fuck slowly up into her tight heat. Persephone rolls her hips, fucking herself on them, and I need to rip my clothes off. Get them the fuck off.

I bring her to another orgasm before I carry her to our bed.

Persephone rolls over onto her stomach to watch me undress. Her hooded gaze reflects desire and lust and a primal need. I strip everything off as fast as I undressed her. She sits up as I come closer to the bed, then rises to her knees.

"I need you," she says softly, nearly breathlessly, then runs her hands all over my chest. I hold her waist as she explores me, tracing paths down to my hips, then taking my cock in one fist.

Persephone uses her other hand to push me a step away from the bed, and then she slides down to the floor, to her knees, and takes me into her mouth.

Fuck me. The sight of her is everything.

My head tips back at the feeling of her tongue on my crown. She teases me.

She takes me deep, the pleasure forcing my toes to curl.

Threading my fingers through her hair, I hold her head and guide her mouth onto me, letting her hold my hips, letting her suck while I fuck into her mouth. It is every sensation I have ever wanted. I could spend eternity doing this.

My cock pulses. I need to come, but not in her throat. Not yet. I've barely just gotten started.

"Inside you," I say, my voice rough. "I want to come inside you."

I pull her to her feet and kiss her onto the bed. Persephone spreads her legs wide underneath me and arches her body to mine.

There's no better sight than her face, blushed from her orgasms, and her eyes half-lidded with pleasure and her lips parted to pant my name.

"Come inside me," she says. "Please, my king. Please. I need you."

Ravenously, I find her opening and thrust in. In one swift motion I'm buried to the hilt, and her nails dig in my back as she cries out in pleasure.

I fuck her relentlessly, chasing both of our orgasms. The bed creaks with each thrust and the headboard bangs against the wall. Over and over, I take her. Mercilessly and savagely fucking my queen.

We both moan as we come together and I rest beside her. Our breathing is labored but even still, I kiss her neck and her shoulders, and she rolls over to meet my lips with hers. I have been empty without this. Empty and lonely, no matter how I tried to live in the moment.

"More," she whispers, and at her command, my hard cock meets her entrance and I do her bidding. Urged by lust, I rock into her and love how her back arches when I brush against her clit with the angle of my thrust.

I can see nothing as I pull my hips back and push forward. Back and then forward. Persephone meets my strokes, her pussy tightening and tightening. She slips her hand between us, her fingers seeking out her clit, and rubs herself to another orgasm that coats me in her pleasure.

Fuck me, the sight of her pleasure is intoxicating. I pray I remember this sight for all of my life. I capture her mouth and fuck her senselessly. My body is coming alive again. My muscles tense and my skin is hot. I have made efforts at keeping myself awake through these cycles of the moon, but it's only now that I feel every muscle again. Every sensation. Every bit of her heat. Every breath.

But mostly I feel her.

My queen is fit to me. She was *made* for me. Fated for me. The tight hold of her pussy must be proof of this. I will give my pleasure to her without hesitation.

Her hands curl around my neck, and she pulls me closer, kissing me harder. Her nails scrape against my skin and I love it. The sharp points of her teeth nip at my lip. Persephone writhes beneath me.

I smooth her hair back from her face, moving my hips slowly, the urge to come as strong as I have ever felt it. "What is it, my queen? What?"

"Turn *over*." Persephone pushes at my shoulders, and I roll onto my back, bringing her with me.

She sinks down on me, arching her back, and drags her nails over my chest. Fucking hell, she's delectable and her desire for control is heady.

"Like this," she gasps, and circles her hips. "Like this. I want you to come like this. While I ride you."

My fingers dig into the flesh of her hips, and I guide

her on my hard cock. Persephone moans, folding forward to wriggle her hips onto me, then arches back again. She comes *again*, insatiable, then looks down at me with a glint in her eyes.

"You look…as if…" It's more work for her to ride me, but she does it beautifully. Persephone puts all of her body into each movement, going down as far as she can, throwing her head back. "As if you might come."

I thrust up, pulling her down at the same time, then do it again. Persephone gasps, her pussy beginning to flutter around me. I find her clit with the pad of my thumb and circle it relentlessly, thrusting as I do.

Persephone tries to stay in control as she rides, but she melts under my touch, the circles of her hips trembling. I'm on the edge of losing myself inside her.

She parts her lips and cries out as her orgasm races through her. I pull her down, buried in her as deeply as I can get.

My release is so intense that I cannot tell I am shouting. I only know it is me after a few minutes, when another surge comes and my voice falters with it. The pleasure seems to last forever. It is the longest release I have ever had, and it erases some of the loneliness I have felt. It makes those moon cycles seem as though they passed in hours, not weeks.

Everything is more intense.

Persephone bends down with my cock still inside her. She kisses my neck and my cheek and my lips as I come down.

It takes a long time. Persephone is so warm and soft in my arms, and my release was *so* strong, that my vision stays dark for a while. I run my hands over her back, tracing the line of her spine, then run my fingers through her hair.

When I can finally see again, Persephone is smiling down at me, her face pink and her hair tangled, radiant and satisfied and completely at peace.

"Hello," she says softly, brushing her fingers through my hair.

"Hello, my queen," I say, and kiss her again.

We kiss like we have all the time there ever was in all the realms. When we finally break away, Persephone laughs with a happy sigh.

"I missed you."

"And I you."

epilogue

THE FIRE BEFORE ME IS WARM AND BRIGHT, roaring in the grate. It doesn't matter that the days have been growing longer so gradually. We have such strong firelight that our rooms are lit with the warmth of the flames.

With nothing but comfort, I lounge on a sofa before the fire, leaning against my king, his arm around me and a book in my lap. It's pages are worn and the cover is a leather binding with no name.

It's the book Silvie brought for me. I have studied it, little by little, during this year's moon cycles with my king. I've taken each word, and each sentence, and each spell slowly, letting them sink into my mind and bloom there while we go about our days. The grimoires in the Underworld are ancient magic, some lost to those in Olympus, and I will return it.

In winter, the days are shorter in the Underworld as well. That means we have more time to walk the paths and tend to the various places throughout the realm. It means there is a slower pace to all that happens, so when we meet a soul in the realms, there is no rush. We can pause and speak to them for as long as we wish.

Many more souls speak with Hades now. Silvie has told me that he was not so open before he took me as his queen. He did not spend much time at all coming to know the souls who dwell in his realms. He was lonely, Silvie will admit if I press, but he absorbed himself in his work and his duties and did not reach out to find connections.

Now, we have found a balance. There are sessions at court and meetings with advisers. There are walks among the realms with Cerberus and without him. There are places to visit to ensure they remain in good repair. There are souls to speak with. There are chances each day to break bread with others. There are celebrations in Elysium and peace in the meadows.

And there are quiet evenings alone. There are the meals we linger over, taking a blanket and glasses of wine to the floor in front of the sofa, sharing grapes and sweets until we cannot keep our hands off one another and must go to bed.

Or at least we must clear away the food so that it is not crushed in the midst of our passion.

Then there are moments like this, when we are together in the quiet warmth. Our souls resting on one another. Hades enjoys looking into the fire to allow his mind to wander, and I like to read my books. I will carry the knowledge with me when I return to Olympus, but it is not only the spells themselves I will use. It is the theories behind them. This book speaks to the magic that surrounds us in the Underworld. It describes a world of spells and magic, but it also describes how a witch—or a goddess—might prepare her mind to interact with such powers.

There is light and there is darkness within us all. Both sides are required for the flawed ways in which we exist. Which is a blessing. Gratitude should exist for every piece of us. Including the side we were taught to fear or feel shame for. In contrary, we should love it and allow that power to rise all the same.

That is what I would like to improve upon. I am confident in my powers in all the realms, but there is always more to know. There is always something to understand in a deeper way.

Now that I have time to understand and not fear losing my magic, I'm determined to learn it all. To study with Hecate on our long journeys.

That seems to be a duty of a queen—a deep understanding of her realm, and the souls within, and the magic everywhere. Hades shifts next to me, letting out a breath.

This past hour has been peaceful and quiet, but we are both ignoring the fact of today.

"My love," he says and wraps his hand around my

arm, running it slowly up and down. It is not a desperate touch. It is a comfortable one, as if we still have many moon cycles together.

I turn my head toward him. "Yes?"

"It is time for you to leave me soon."

He reaches over and rests his fingers underneath my chin, turning me a little farther so he can kiss me. It is as electrifying as it was the first time, burning just as bright. It thrills me. There is a sense of danger in it, though he is not dangerous to me. Perhaps I am only sensing the greatness of our powers together. We could be dangerous, but we are not.

That strength could come out in the bed. In our passion. Warmth pools between my legs. I squeeze my thighs together and deepen the kiss, opening my mouth so he can explore me.

I come up for breath after a while, my heart racing from the kiss. My book remains open in my lap. I move to close it, but then…

"Not yet," I decide. "It can be a longer winter this year."

He smirks at me, his eyes darkening, more of the firelight reflected there. "I so enjoy the longer winters."

Hades takes the book from my hands and sets it aside, then scoops me up in his arms and carries me across the room to our bed. I put my arms around his neck and pull him close to kiss the corner of his mouth.

When we reach the bed, he stops at the side to kiss me again before he lowers me down. The bed is soft underneath me. It calls to me, the way the Underworld calls to me when I am away. I do not want to let go of Hades, so I don't, and it is some time before he can pull away, laughing.

"It will happen," I remind him, lest he think he can distract me enough to keep me here all through summer. "The winter will go. The spring will come again. There is no escaping it, Hades. The new season *will* come."

"I know it, my queen." He leans down and kisses me again, his hand sliding underneath my dress, ready to take it off for me. Ready to expose my skin to him so he can tease my nipples and slide his tongue over all of his favorite places. I am about to lose track of time—I know that for certain. It is impossible to keep track when my king is with me this way. "But not yet."

The Seduction of the Gods world is far from over, I have so
many more stories planned and I can't wait for you to read
them! If you want to be the first to hear about new books
in this world when they're available, sign up below!

about w winters

Thank you so much for reading my romances. I'm just
a stay at home mom and avid reader turned author
and I couldn't be happier.

I hope you love my books as much as I do!

More by Willow Winters
WWW.WILLOWWINTERSWRITES.COM/BOOKS